DANCING ON THE DRIVE

THE BACHELOR NEXT DOOR - BOOK TWO

PAMELA FORD

AINE PRESS

BOOKS BY PAMELA FORD

BACHELOR NEXT DOOR SERIES

Love on the Lane

Dancing on the Drive

Breathless on the Boulevard

Romance on the Road

Kissing on the Corner

CONTINENTAL BREAKFAST CLUB SERIES

Over Easy

Fresh Brewed

Honey Glazed

OUT OF IRELAND SERIES

To Ride a White Horse

A Rush of White Wings

No part of this book may be used or reproduced in any manner whatsoever without written permission except in the case of brief quotations embodied in critical articles and reviews.

This is a work of fiction. Names, characters, places, and incidents are either the products of the author's imagination or are used fictitiously. Any resemblance to actual events, locales, organizations or persons, living or dead, is entirely coincidental.

A previous version of this book was published under the title, *The Wedding Heiress*.

DANCING ON THE DRIVE
Copyright © 2008, 2017 by Pamela Ford
All rights reserved
ISBN: 978-1-944792-03-9

Excerpt from *Breathless on the Boulevard*
Copyright © 2007, 2017 by Pamela Ford

Cover design by Robbi Strandemo

 Created with Vellum

*To my daughters, Margaux, Ella and Laurel, who know that
life well-lived is filled with laughter.*

1

———

Delaney McBride knew her fortunes had changed the moment the telephone rang. She danced across the room to take the call she'd been waiting for all afternoon, the one that would put her back in control of her life. She paused to compose herself, then said in her most businesslike voice, "Delaney McBride."

"Pumpkin. How the hell are you?"

Her brain stopped. Her heart stilled. Suddenly she was the fat, orange-haired teenager who'd obsessed over Mike Connery all her life. The high-school junior who'd pressed a note into Mike's hand that said she would *save* herself for him. Her face began to burn. Thank God she and her mother had moved out of town a few months later.

"Pumpkin?"

She dropped into the soft leather cushion of her living room sofa and pressed a hand to her cheek, the heat warming her palm. How could something she'd done fifteen years ago have such an effect on her today? This call was supposed to be a job offer, not a connection to a past she'd rather forget. She tried to pull her thoughts into order. "Yes?"

"This is Mike Connery from—"

"Birch Harbor. I know." The words came out more sharply than she intended. Surely he wasn't calling about the will.

"I'm sorry about your great-aunt. She was a wonderful woman."

A sympathy call from Mike Connery? "Thanks, she was really special."

"Uh, I'm calling about her will."

There it was. She exhaled. Well, why *wouldn't* he call? He stood to gain—or lose—as much as anyone else. For a moment, she felt a peculiar camaraderie with him, swept into the maelstrom of her aunt's eccentricity by the woman's last will.

She shoved a hand through her hair as if to shove the emotion away. "I can't believe this will is legal," she said. "I've never heard of anything so absurd. I even met with another lawyer ..."

"I'm an attorney, Pumpy. It's ironclad."

Her stomach tightened. She wasn't Pumpy anymore. Pumpkin and her insecurities no longer existed, thanks to years of therapy. She wanted to tell Mike to call her Delaney, but couldn't bring herself to let on that the old nickname bothered her. She made a fist, then let out a controlled laugh. "So my attorney confirmed," she said in a low voice. "Although, as a lawyer you should know nothing is ever ironclad if you have the right connections."

Mike gave an equally controlled chuckle. "Does that

mean we shouldn't count on you? I'll tell the other heirs so they can quit planning ..."

"Planning?"

"Yeah. To pay off credit cards, take their first vacation in years, have an operation. Sully Sullivan was going back to Ireland to see his mother. Hasn't seen her in twenty-five years, and she's getting old."

"Is this why you're calling? To pressure me into complying with that ridiculous will? To guilt me into overseeing a bunch of weddings?" Delaney stood and crossed the living room of her Victorian row house to gaze out at the organic food store across the street. She'd chosen to live in Boston's South End because it was full of young professionals, people with drive and an eye on the future. Her lifestyle was totally incongruous with wedding planning.

He ignored her questions. "Are you in or not?"

God knew she needed the hundred thousand dollars her great-aunt had left her. She'd been unemployed for more than three months, laid off when the ad agency where she worked lost the big account she was in charge of.

Now she was in debt up to her eyeballs. Her savings were depleted, her rent was due, her car payment was overdue, the balance on her credit card kept going up, and all she had to live on was a small unemployment check. The mere thought of her finances made her heart begin to race. She sucked in a breath to calm herself.

"Pumpkin?"

All of which made this inheritance a godsend. Except, in order to get the money, which she desperately needed, she had to go to back to her hometown in Wisconsin—Birch

Harbor. Worse, she had to finish planning the weddings that remained on the books of her late aunt's wedding planning shop.

"Are you in or out?" Mike pressed.

"It's not that simple."

"What's the problem? You have an aversion to money?" he asked with thinly disguised impatience.

She huffed. She was supposed to be getting a job offer today from an ad agency in San Francisco. With a salary nearly rivaling what she'd receive from her inheritance—and no requirement that she had to plan weddings to get paid.

If she'd only heard from them already, this whole conversation would be unnecessary. "Of course not. It's just, I'm not sure I have the time to take this on. I don't know anything about wedding planning."

"You don't have to be incredible at it, just good enough to—"

"And frankly, I'm not into that happily-ever-after scene."

Mike laughed out loud. "Seems to me you were quite the hopeless romantic in your day."

Every possible thought in her head vaporized. For a moment she couldn't speak. What kind of man would bring up her old infatuation with him to win an argument? She forced herself to say something, anything. "Yes, well, I've long since learned the error of my ways."

He made a choking sound. "So you'd give up a hundred thousand bucks because you don't want to plan a few weddings? Hell, for a hundred grand, I'd clean out horse stalls barehanded. And I'd smile the whole time."

"Therein lies the difference between us, now, doesn't it," she said with a sniff.

"We're talking about a few months, not a lifetime. So what is it really? You don't need the money? You can't get a leave from your job?"

"I can take off whenever I want." With no job at all, taking time off wasn't an issue, but she wasn't about to open her whole life to him. She'd already spent enough years being a loser in Mike Connery's eyes. She opened the front door and stepped outside, pausing at the top of the steep concrete steps. A cool spring breeze slid over her bare arms.

"What's the big deal, then? You afraid to fail? Or afraid to try?"

"I just told you."

He laughed out loud, a long laugh that took her straight back to high school—and irritated her to no end. They were talking to each other with the same friendly antagonism they'd had in childhood, as though fifteen years hadn't even passed.

"Oh, I get it. You have a boyfriend."

"No, I don't."

"You're so in love you don't want to leave Boston."

"You're full of crap." Her voice went up a notch and she grasped the stair rail. God, but he was the same old Mike. A year older than she and always had to win the arguments. Didn't matter if the sky was blue; he'd argue that it was pink until he won. No wonder he'd become a lawyer.

She heard the beep of an incoming call and pulled the phone away from her ear to check Caller ID. *Yes!* It was the ad agency she'd been waiting to hear from. *With her job offer.*

She grinned. Thank God her cousin Nora had passed Delaney's resume on to an ad exec she knew in San Francisco. Because that little connection was about to guarantee there would be no wedding planning in Delaney's future. "Mike, I have to call you back. I've got a business call on the other line."

She swiped to the new call without waiting for his reply. "Delaney McBride," she said in a professional voice that revealed none of her excitement.

Mike was so wrong about her. No boyfriend would ever prevent her from doing something she wanted to do. That described her mother, and she would never be like her mother—always needing a man to rely on, always thinking a man would make everything better. And then never getting the man.

Five minutes later she felt more like her mother than she ever had in her life. All dressed up and nowhere to go. Reaching for the brass ring and missing once again. She stared out her front window without seeing anything. They'd offered the job to someone else. Someone with more experience. Someone who was a *better fit*.

Whatever that meant. When all was said and done, she just hadn't been good enough.

She glanced at her watch without knowing why. There was no place she needed to be; she had no meetings, no conference calls, no appointments, no deadlines. She wanted to bang her head against a wall. How could she have lost complete control of her life? She had no job. She had no money. She had no prospects. *She had no choices*. None except go to Birch Harbor and get up to her elbows in white satin, butter-cream frosting, and rosebud bouquets.

Seriously Aunt Ellie? She loved the woman dearly, but what had ever made her think this was a good idea?

"I can't do it, I can't go back there," she said to the empty room, knowing full well that was exactly what she had to do—at least until a good job offer came her way.

The thought of calling Mike back sent a tremor through her stomach.

Not yet. Soon. She'd call soon. Just not yet.

She wondered whether his teenaged good looks had matured into handsome. Whether he was still as lean and fit as when he had been playing high-school baseball. Whether his brown hair was prematurely peppered with white like his father's had been. And whether his blue eyes could still make her heart pound.

Are you afraid? he'd asked a few minutes ago.

Afraid? Damn right she was afraid. But it wasn't wedding planning she was afraid of.

———

Mike rounded the door of his law office to find his friend, Dan Hobart, kicked back in the black leather desk chair, work boots up on the cherrywood desk, fingers laced behind his head. Though his blue mechanic's jumpsuit looked completely out of place in the professionally appointed office, Dan's demeanor was that of a full partner. Mike leaned against the doorway and grinned. "Anything I can get to make you more comfortable, Hobes?" he asked.

"How about a massage therapist?" Dan grinned, then pulled his feet off the desk and sat up. "I had to drop Bill

Brighton's car off for him so thought I'd stop in before I head back to the shop. You talk to Pumpkin?"

Mike nodded. "You know how she used to be that tagalong, the gnat we were always trying to get rid of? Well, now she's morphed into a giant pain-in-the-ass."

"No go, huh?"

"Yeah. Said she'd call me back, but I'm not holding out a lot of hope."

"We should have left her tied to that maple tree when she was eight."

Despite his irritation, Mike laughed. He could still see chubby Pumpkin McBride loosely tied to that tree, her mop of unruly orange hair blowing into her face as he and Dan assured her this really was how you played Arthur, and they'd be back in five minutes. Three hours later, it had taken a Hershey bar and the seventy-two cents they pooled between them to keep her from tattling. "Could be she wants revenge because I hit her with an arrow that time we were playing William Tell," he said.

"It was only a foam arrow," Dan said. "I can't believe she'd still be holding that against you."

"For some reason, I suspect her memory may be long."

"Maybe she didn't like that snowman we made in her front yard—the one where we put a real pumpkin on top for the head." He started to chuckle, then quickly sobered. "It was just stupid kid stuff. She has to know that. So what do you think's the problem?"

"I don't know." Mike shoved his hands in the pockets of his khakis. "Maybe she doesn't need the money."

"Doesn't she care that the rest of us do?" Dan took a

drink from the coffee cup Mike had left on the desk an hour ago. He grimaced. "Yech. Cold."

"Doesn't sound like it. I played all the guilt cards. Even told her Sully wanted to go back to Ireland to see his mother."

Dan snorted out a laugh. "You nabbed the plot from *Going My Way*? What if she's seen the movie?"

"It was a spur of the moment strategy. I just couldn't believe anyone would seriously consider giving up a hundred grand no matter what clause was attached to it." He collapsed into one of the upholstered chairs opposite his desk.

"She understands she's not the only heir that has to do something, right?" Dan asked. "That we have to restore the '57 Chevy. That other people have to—"

"She got a copy of the will."

Dan stood and walked across the office, then turned back to Mike. "The way I see it, you only have one choice."

"Me?"

"Yeah, you. She was always in love with you."

Mike let out a hearty laugh. "Not anymore."

"You can get it back—women never forget their first loves. Play to that attraction and you'll get her to sign on. Once she's knee-deep in wedding planning, you can slip away, no one the wiser. Then we can all get our inheritances and live happily ever after."

"I've got news for you. She's not into that *happily ever after scene*," Mike said, standing. "Her words. Not mine."

Dan clapped him on the back. "Well, then, you're just the man to change her mind."

The office phone jangled and Dan leaned over to pick it

up. "Connery Law Office. How can we help you?" he said cheerfully. His eyes narrowed. "Can I tell him who's calling?" One hand over the mouthpiece, he raised his eyebrows and whispered, "Pumpkin. Be nice. *Really* nice."

Mike put the phone to his ear and sat on the edge of the desk. "Hey, Pumpkin, thanks for calling back," he said in the friendliest voice he could muster. "Dan and I were just talking about all the fun we three used to have."

Dan rolled his eyes.

Silence greeted him from the other end of the line. Maybe he'd gone too far. "Pumpy?"

"Okay," she said. "I've, ah, thought the whole thing over and decided to, ah ... that it would be worthwhile for me to give wedding planning a try. Do one or two weddings and—"

"That's great!"

"So I cleared my schedule for a few weeks."

"Everyone will be happy to hear this." Mike gave Dan a thumbs-up.

Dan twirled his index finger in the air. "Play it up," he whispered.

"I mean, *I'm* happy to hear this," Mike added hastily. "Can't wait to see you. When will you get here?"

"I'm driving, so it'll be a couple of days. Is Sunday soon enough?" she asked less than enthusiastically.

Dan rocked a few celebratory hip-hop moves.

Mike ignored him. "The first wedding is less than two weeks away, so the sooner the better. I'll have someone open the apartment above your great-aunt's wedding shop so it'll be ready for you to move in."

"Thanks, that'll be great. So, um, guess I'll see you … soon."

"Looking forward to it." Yeah, right. What he was looking forward to was getting this whole thing out of the way and his life returning to normal. He hung up the phone and pointed at his friend. "Houston, we have liftoff. She's going to try a wedding or two."

Dan froze. "One or two? She's got to do the whole job."

"One step at a time. At least she's coming to town."

"Yeah, but none of us gets our inheritances unless everyone fulfills the terms of the will. If we lose Pumpkin, we all lose."

"We won't lose her."

"There's only one way to be sure of that." Dan's lips curved up like the Cheshire cat.

"Oh, no. Don't look at me."

"Oh, yes. It's only for a couple of months. She always liked you."

Mike stared at Dan a long moment, then dropped into a chair, shaking his head. "I don't want to lead her on—"

"I'm not saying to seduce her. Just keep our sweet Pumpkin happy so she doesn't quit before all the weddings are finished."

Much as he didn't like what Dan was saying, his friend had a point. "I think this'll take more than just me being nice," he said. "If we really want to make sure everyone gets their inheritance, Pumpkin included, we're both going to have to be nicer to Pumpy than we were in high school."

"Of course. But especially you."

2

———

Delaney walked slowly across the worn hardwood floor of Ellie Clark's Storybook Weddings shop. She had never seen so much white in one place in all her life. White satin, white lace, white netting, white garters, shoes, stockings, candles, favors, guest books ... Aargh. Everywhere she turned it was white, white, white, white, white.

And for what? The pursuit of the everlasting fairytale? Had anyone ever bothered to ask Cinderella how she liked living with her in-laws five years after the wedding? Or whether Snow White still awoke with a smile from Prince Charming's kisses?

Storybook weddings indeed.

She glanced at Lauren Hobart, Ellie's assistant, standing at the work counter, one hand resting on her very pregnant belly, the other flipping through the pages of a big, old-fashioned ledger book. With her blond ponytail and quick smile, she was as cute today as she had been in high school.

Lauren grinned for about the tenth time in ten minutes.

"I'm so happy you're here. Even when Mike told us you were coming, I was afraid you'd change your mind at the last minute. Say you didn't need the money or something."

Not need a hundred thousand dollars? Hardly. Delaney picked up a clear glass slipper from the shelf and peered through it at eye level. Who bought this stuff?

Dumb question. The cottage crowd, of course. Though, she'd be hard-pressed to call the big homes rising up along the lake *cottages* anymore. The only reason such an unusual wedding shop could survive so far away from a major metropolitan area was that Birch Harbor was a favorite vacation spot. Like the rest of the towns in Door County, its downtown was filled with quaint boutiques, fudge shops, and antique stores. All of which enhanced its charm and made it an ideal location for romantic destination weddings.

Delaney set the slipper back on the shelf and ran a hand down a swath of white satin. Five weddings. She just had to finish the planning and execution of five May and June weddings—all that remained on the books—to get her inheritance. Even though she'd told Mike she would give it a try by doing a couple of weddings, she'd known all along she would do them all. She needed the money too badly.

Self-doubt roiled her mind, a rather common occurrence ever since she'd received the call about the inheritance from Great-Uncle Joe, Ellie's brother.

She turned to Lauren. "I still don't understand why Ellie wrote her will this way. I know nothing about wedding planning. This weekend's bride could discover her special day has become an epic disaster under my management."

Lauren let out a laugh. "That's pretty unlikely. Ellie took care of almost everything already—catering, flowers, the band, alterations, you name it." She ran a finger down the open ledger, then looked up at Delaney. "You just need to make sure everything happens on Saturday when it's supposed to."

Delaney moved to stand beside Lauren and scan the page. Names, phone numbers, contacts, details—it was all in the book. Aunt Ellie may not have progressed to computerized record-keeping, but at least she was totally organized. She worried her lower lip. She'd never run from a challenge before, no reason to start now. As long as she applied the principles of effective management, she should be able to pull this off.

Probably. Maybe. Perhaps.

"I'm so glad you decided to come," Lauren said. "For a while I thought I was going to have to make these weddings happen myself—with a two-year-old at home and a baby due in a couple of weeks and a doctor who keeps telling me to take it easy. Like that's possible with Kristian, anyway. He has more energy than any toddler I've ever seen."

"Thank God Ellie didn't schedule a wedding every weekend." Otherwise Delaney thought she might have a mental breakdown on the spot. "I just don't get it. Why did she write this will? What am I doing here?"

"Well ... you want to make sure five couples enter wedded bliss in the most romantic way possible."

Delaney held back from rolling her eyes. "No."

Lauren closed the book and tilted her head thoughtfully. "You love the idea of making fairytales come true—white doves, white horses, white swans—"

"No." The horror of her situation began to sink in.

White doves and swans? Glass slippers? Golden carriages? She was actually going to do this?

"Hmm." Lauren stared at her for a long moment, then scrunched up her face. "Well, there's always the inheritance."

Delaney grinned.

"You're only doing this for the money?" Lauren's brow furrowed.

"Well, yeah. Why else would I do it?"

'To help people get a wedding day they'll never forget. To send them out into their new lives surrounded by magic." She opened her arms wide. "I just love this shop."

Oh, God, Lauren was one of those romantics. Delaney brushed her shoulder-length hair behind her ear. What exquisite irony. She, the one in charge, was only doing this for an inheritance. But her assistant was a googly-eyed romantic.

"You know what I think?" Lauren lifted a spangle-studded wedding tiara off a display, set it on her head, and fluffed the attached veil over her shoulders. She spun in a circle. "I think that once you've done a couple of weddings, you'll find romance has gotten into your heart and under your skin. You'll want to give up advertising for the enchanted world of fairytale wedding planning."

Delaney shook her head. Hopeless. Absolutely hopeless. Maybe even delusional. It was going to be a long couple of months.

Lauren snatched up a bouquet of blush-and-cream silk roses and thrust it into Delaney's hands. "Hold this a minute." Then she pulled the tiara off her own head and plopped it onto Delaney's, smoothing the waist-length veil down the back. She clasped her hands together. "Oh, Delaney, with your red hair you could be a model!"

She turned Delaney toward the wall mirror. "Now, doesn't that make you feel even a bit romantic?"

A bell tinkled at the front door and two handsome thirty-something men stepped inside, both wearing dirty jeans and sweatshirts, both carrying themselves with the easy self-assurance of accomplished athletes.

"You remember Dan and Mike, don't you?" Lauren danced across the shop floor to share a quick kiss with the taller of the two, obviously her husband, Dan.

Though it had been fifteen years since Delaney had seen either man, it was easy to see the boys they had been in the men they had become. Memories of adolescence crowded her mind, and she purposely focused her attention on Dan. He was over six feet tall and more than a few pounds heavier than high school, but he had the same impish grin and, no doubt, the same mischievous personality.

"Is this our new wedding planner?" Mike asked.

Delaney finally let herself look at him. Mike Connery. Shorter than Dan, but still lean and fit, his jaw still strong and, yeah, just as she'd suspected, a few early streaks of silver in his brown hair. Suddenly, words of advice her grandmother had shared at her grandfather's funeral popped into her mind: *Just don't search so far and wide you miss out on the bachelor next door.*

Seriously? *Yeah. No. Been there, done that with this guy, Grandma. Not going there again.*

"Yes! This is our wedding planner!" Lauren gestured expressively with both hands.

Only then did Delaney remember the veil. She snatched it off her head, her eyes locking with Mike's just long enough for a sigh to catch in her throat. Damn, but those blue eyes could still wrap her in their spell. She crumpled the veil in her fist.

———

Mike tried to hide his shock. This was Pumpkin? Little, round, red-haired pumpkin was now ... Hell, in her tight jeans and clingy T-shirt, it was easy to see they'd never be calling her Plumpy Pumpy again.

"Welcome back!" Dan stuck out a hand, then changed his mind and hugged her. "You look great. Mike, doesn't she look great?"

"Yeah. I almost didn't recognize you." Lame. He could feel Dan's hand in the small of his back propelling him forward. He took a step toward Pumpkin and gave her an awkward hug.

She broke the contact after a second. "Hi, Mike. Dan," she said, not smiling. "Nice to see you again."

"So what are you two boys doing here?" Lauren quickly asked. "Don't you have cars to fix?"

"We wanted to say hi to Pumpkin," Dan said.

Cars to fix? They were still working on cars? She frowned at Mike. "I thought you were a lawyer."

"Lawyer. Mechanic. What's the difference?" Dan smiled. "They both make the world go round."

Delaney looked from one to the other. "Seriously, what do you guys do?"

"We're mechanics," Mike said just as Dan said, "We're lawyers."

"Stop it, you two." Lauren slapped Dan's arm. "Mike's a lawyer. Dan took over his dad's shop when he retired a couple of years ago."

"I'm not just a pretty boy," Mike added. "I'm a mechanic, too."

Delaney looked at Dan, her brow furrowed.

"He was hanging around the shop so much when he moved back to town, I took pity on him and gave him a job," Dan explained.

"Pity? You couldn't find help as good with cars as I am."

"Part-time," Dan said. "Really part-time. It makes him feel useful."

Mike grinned. "We just moved your aunt's '57 Chevy into the shop and I was checking it over to see what needs fixing."

"They've been coveting that car forever," Lauren said. "Now they're like two kids who've taken over the candy store."

"Once we get it running, Mike will take you for a drive. That convertible top makes it great for spins in the moonlight," Dan said.

Mike cleared his throat. No master of subtlety, Dan. "We actually did stop by to talk about something other than cars," he said. "We have an idea. Since all the heirs have to succeed for any of us to inherit, we want to hold regular meetings. Once a week until the deadline."

"Follow each other's progress. Cheer each other on. Listen to tapes of motivational speakers," Dan said.

Delaney's hazel eyes widened, and Mike figured she

was trying to figure out how much to believe of what Dan was saying.

"It's best to ignore him most of the time," Mike said. "Makes life easier. Anyway, we're thinking of holding the first one tomorrow night. At seven. In the public meeting room at the library."

"Do you really think we need meetings?" Delaney asked.

For a moment no one replied, everyone probably as surprised as he was that she didn't simply agree. The Pumpkin he used to know would have just gone along with the idea, no questions asked.

"Well, it's a nice way to support each other. And you can meet all the heirs," Lauren offered.

"But I just got into town and—"

"Monday's the only night that worked for everyone," Dan said.

"I'm not sure about taking the time. I'll have a lot to do before Saturday's—"

"Your aunt has this wedding pretty tightly organized." Lauren gave an encouraging smile.

Delaney shook her head. "I don't know. It seems sort of unnecessary. I mean, isn't the money motivation enough for everyone?"

Odd thing to say, considering she'd already made the point that it wasn't enough motivation for her. Pumpkin's lack of commitment was the main reason they'd decided to hold heirs' meetings. "Even if you don't need meetings, I think they would be helpful for the rest of us," Mike said. 'To keep everyone committed."

Delaney looked at him with an expression he couldn't

read. The Pumpkin of old had never been able to hide her feelings about anything—her face always gave her away and her heart was always on her sleeve.

"I guess we can try one meeting," she finally said.

Try. There was that word again.

Dan caught his eye and nodded almost imperceptibly. Mike knew exactly what his friend was saying—*try* wasn't good enough. It was time to kick the Pumpkin Project into high gear.

Long after Mike and Dan had left, Delaney kept thinking about the conversation. She'd come to town hoping she could quietly take care of the weddings and then leave. She didn't want to get involved here, and especially didn't want Mike to think she'd spent years pining for him.

Because she hadn't.

But the moment she set eyes on him in the wedding shop, she'd realized how easily she could become attracted to him again. And she was in no mood for unattainable adolescent fantasies. Which was why she hadn't wanted to go to the heirs' meeting. As silly as it sounded, she knew the less time she spent around Mike the better off she'd be. Still, she understood why the other heirs might want to get together.

A sigh escaped her. Fine, she would go. But she'd be the last one in the door and the first one out.

3

Monday night at seven, Mike took a seat at the old wooden conference table in the library meeting room with the rest of Ellie Clark's heirs. Reality smacked him in the face. In order for each of them to get their inheritance, every person in this group had to accomplish the task they were assigned in the will. Damn, but this would be one hell of an undertaking.

He'd listed the heirs and each of their assignments on the whiteboard, figuring they could have a brief, motivational discussion. He'd also asked the executor to distribute a checklist and discuss what would constitute *success*—especially with regard to the weddings. But other than those two topics, he had no real agenda planned.

Henry "Sully" Sullivan and Henry "Stonewall" Jackson were sitting across from one another, arms crossed over their chests, not speaking. The men, both in their early seventies, had played in a trio with Ellie's late husband, Henry Clark, for many years. Now, the two remaining Henrys had to oversee the building of a new band shell at the park, the cost of which would be covered by funds Ellie had earmarked for the purpose. Then the two had to put together a summer Friday-night concert series called Music in the Park—and be the opening act for the first concert.

"How are you guys doing tonight?" Mike asked. They answered with unintelligible grunts.

Not good. Not good at all. Though their common first name brought the three Henrys together years ago, Sully and Stonewall had always been like oil and vinegar. Henry Clark had been the stabilizing force, the one who was able to keep the peace. Once he died, the other two had drifted apart. Mike ran a hand through his hair. Somehow, these two had to set aside their differences long enough to get the job done.

He and Dan probably had the easiest task—restoring Henry Clark's old Chevy and driving it in the Fourth of July parade. If all went according to plan, they would get the title to the car and fifty thousand dollars each.

"It's past seven," Dan leaned over to mutter. "And no Pumpkin."

Mike glanced at his watch. Hopefully, she hadn't changed her mind about coming tonight. He was sure Pumpkin would become more vested in the outcome if she made a personal connection with the rest of the heirs. "Let's give her a little more time. Maybe she's just running late."

After another five minutes, he gave up. "I guess we might as well get started."

"Without our wedding planner?" Sully asked.

Mike shrugged. "You all know Ed Snyder." He gestured at a stout middle-aged man sitting at the head of the table. "I asked him to come tonight because he was Ellie's lawyer and he's the executor."

"I've never liked that term." Stonewall pulled on one of his long gray eyebrows. "Sounds like he's supposed to kill people."

"Maybe he could start with you," Sully muttered.

Mike studied the two silver-haired men and wondered for a moment how well his patience would hold out over the next few months. "Now, guys—"

"Actually, *executor* isn't used much anymore. The term is usually *personal representative*," Ed said.

Stonewall let out a snort. "That's sort of like calling a janitor a sanitary engineer."

"There's no law that says we have to use either of those titles. We can call him anything we want," Lauren said helpfully.

"That's right," Sully said. "How about we compromise on something like ... *will checker?*"

"Will checker? Sounds like somebody's name." Stonewall extended a hand. "Damn glad to meet you, my name's Will Checker."

"Sometimes you are such a stupid old fool," Sully retorted, his double chin vibrating. "Fine, then you come up with something better."

"I will!" Stonewall pushed back his chair and stood.

The executor held up a hand like a stop sign. "I really think *personal representative* says exactly what—"

"*Heir overseer,*" Stonewall interrupted.

Sully stood defiantly. "*Heir manager.*"

Mike threw an exasperated look at Lauren and Dan,

both of whom were obviously fighting to hold back their laughter. "How about *heir patrol?*" Dan said with a smirk.

"You're not helping." Lauren slapped his arm.

Both Henrys nodded. "I like it," Sully said.

"And our slogan could be ..." a woman's voice said from the doorway. Pumpkin stepped into the room, her red hair curling softly around her face, her hazel eyes twinkling. "Our slogan could be," she repeated, "heir-ly to bed and heir-ly to rise makes a man healthy, wealthy and wise. Seems appropriate."

Mike stood, smiling. "This, everyone, is our new wedding planner—"

"Delaney McBride," Lauren chimed in. "Delaney, these are the Henrys and the execu—personal rep—the guy who's going to oversee the will." Lauren introduced each man by name, and Pumpkin went around the table shaking hands before taking a seat.

Stonewall frowned and plopped back into his chair. "So let's not get carried away here. We don't need a slogan."

"*Heir patrol* is enough." Sully sat down, too.

"Let's get on with this," Stonewall said. "I don't have all night to sit around here jawing."

Mike held back from pointing out that this inane discussion had been started by Stonewall himself.

"Sorry I'm late," Delaney said. "I just got off a long conversation with a bride about whether her guests should throw confetti or rice after the ceremony."

"What did she decide?" Lauren asked, leaning forward.

"Confetti. Turquoise and peach to go with her exotic island theme."

Mike cleared his throat to get everyone's attention

again. "Since all of us have to achieve something in order for any of us to get our inheritance, I thought it would help if we regularly got together to see how we're doing."

"Don't we need to vote on *heir patrol?*" Sully asked.

Oh hell. "Sure, why not? All in favor of *heir patrol* say *aye.*"

"I don't believe that adhered to Robert's Rules of Order," Stonewall said.

"We probably don't have to be so formal," Ed offered.

"Maybe we should vote on it." Delaney smiled sweetly at Mike and crossed her long legs.

Mike forced a smile. "All in favor of Robert's Rules of Order, say *aye.*"

Stonewall's lone *aye* echoed in the large room.

"All opposed say *nay,*" Mike said, following proper Robert's Rules format.

A chorus of *nays* rang out.

One battle over. Might as well close the door on *heir patrol* as long as they were at it. "All in favor of *heir patrol,* say *aye,*" he said.

The two Henrys and Pumpkin chorused *aye.*

Mike cast a sideways glance at Pumpkin. For someone who had been so against fulfilling the terms of her great-aunt's will, she was sure wading in deep. "The motion passes."

"There wasn't a motion," Stonewall pointed out.

Mike fixed his eyes on Stonewall. "It's good enough. Ed Snyder is now officially the *Heir Patrol.* Is it all right with everyone if we get down to business now?"

Stonewall raised his hand. "How are you two doing on that car? Henry and Ellie left it sitting on the tires for years.

I'm sure it can't be driven. You think you'll be finished in eight weeks? Well, seven weeks now."

Dan screwed up his face. "We've ordered all the parts," he said. "It'll be tight, but you don't have to worry about Mike and me. Come hell or high water, we'll meet the deadline."

"I'll second that," Mike said. "Now, let's—"

"And how about the wedding planning?" Stonewall zeroed in on Pumpkin. "There's a wedding this weekend, isn't there?"

She nodded. "We'll be fine. I guess. Just trying to figure out all the pieces. It's a good thing I have Lauren."

"And, we've already been contacted by another potential customer!" Lauren interjected.

"Who we can't possibly take on," Pumpkin said quickly. "We're not in business to get more business. Anyway, Aunt Ellie had things so well organized, this wedding should really be okay."

"Okay?" Lauren chirped. "More than okay! It will be absolutely lovely, a celebration of love to be remembered for a lifetime."

Pumpkin turned slowly to stare at Lauren. "Yeah. That."

Mike pointed at the Henrys. "Okay, guys, you're on. How's the new band shell coming along?"

"That deadline is for the birds. We'll never make it," Stonewall said.

Sully glared at him. "Is the glass ever half-full in that godforsaken life of yours?"

Stonewall rubbed a hand across his jaw. "I'm a realist.

Any idiot with a brain is going to know we won't be able to have a new band shell built by the Fourth of July."

"They can do it on TV in a week," Sully said.

"Reality shows have hundreds of workers—"

"Failure can't be an option," Mike said. "What can we do to help?"

'We don't need help," Stonewall said. "We need time."

"We're doing okay." Sully struggled to his feet. "Stonewall, sometimes you are such a ..."

Stonewall stood and faced his old friend. "Yeah? A what?"

"A—a—boob."

Stonewall's face flushed dark red.

The executor held up a manila folder full of papers. "Henry. And Henry. Ellie knew this might be challenging, so she put together a checklist for each person, to help make it easier."

Mike took the folder and began to hand out the sheets across the table. "Listen up, gentlemen, we have way too much on the line to be getting into it tonight."

"I'm not getting into anything," Stonewall said. "I'm just stating facts."

"Facts," Sully retorted in a raised voice. "You always spin the facts to make your point of view look better."

"Are you calling me a liar?"

"Are you saying you're not?"

"That's it!" Fists raised, Stonewall advanced around the table toward Sully.

"Okay, guys, hold on." Mike lunged out of his seat at the men. Maybe holding meetings wasn't such a good idea after all. These two and their antics wouldn't help convince

Pumpkin to finish all the weddings so everyone could get their inheritance. Instead, she'd probably decide the Henrys would never be able to work together well enough to get their project done, so why even bother.

"This isn't worth an argument!" Pumpkin jumped up and grabbed Stonewall's left forearm just as he let loose with a punch toward Sully that sent her flying.

———

Mike watched Delaney fall as if she were in slow motion. This couldn't be happening. The heirs weren't really exchanging blows in the local library. Delaney stuck her hands out to break her fall and landed with a thud on the thin, industrial carpet. Mike could almost feel the impact reverberate up her arms. She lay still for a second, then moaned and sat up, gingerly holding her left arm. He knelt beside her. "You okay?"

"I don't know. My wrist ..."

"Pumpkin! I'm so sorry," Stonewall said.

She blinked. "Pumpkin?"

"Isn't that what they call you?"

"Some people do." She glared at Mike.

"Maybe she should go to the hospital," Lauren said.

"I'll be fine. Just need some ice." Delaney twisted her wrist to demonstrate how fine she was, then grimaced in pain.

Mike gently prodded the skin around her wrist. "Does that hurt?"

A breath hissed out from between her clenched teeth. "No."

"Liar." He shook his head and admired her grit. "It's swollen already. You're going to the doctor."

"It's not broken."

"How do you know? You get a medical degree since this morning?" He looked up at the rest of the heirs, now bending over them. "Meeting adjourned. I'll take Delaney in. The rest of you go home and write one hundred times, *I will get along with my fellow heirs for the next eight weeks.* We'll reconvene next Monday night. Make sure you take a copy of that sheet I was handing out—and read it."

"I can't come Monday." Sully rested his hands on his T-shirted belly.

"We can't, either." Lauren slid her arm through Dan's. "We're touring the birthing center at the hospital."

"Tuesday's out for me," Stonewall said.

"Don't forget, we have a game Wednesday night," Dan said.

Mike helped Pumpkin to her feet. "We'll make it Thursday, then. Same time, same place."

Half an hour later, he and Delaney were seated in the emergency waiting room. *Emergency waiting*—an oxymoron if he'd ever heard one.

Other than his apology for the Henrys' behavior, they'd hardly spoken since leaving the library. He eyed Pumpkin for obvious signs of pain. Her wrist looked even more swollen. "Still hurt?"

She nodded.

Damn, that couldn't be good. He'd really hoped this would be just a minor—temporary—injury, but his optimism was fading.

"What were you doing trying to jump between two men about to have a fistfight?" he asked irritably.

"If you had kept control of those lunatics, I wouldn't have had to jump anywhere. And what's wrong with you, anyway?" Delaney asked. "I'm the one with the broken wrist."

Sympathy softened his frustration, and he patted her leg. "Maybe it's not broken."

"Yeah. I believe that's what I said when it happened."

"Hopefully this won't make it too hard for you to do the weddings."

Delaney gave a sharp laugh. "I think we can both trust that Lauren will make sure every wedding is a fantasy come true."

"Yeah, well, speaking of fantasies come true ... Remember that paper I was handing out from the executor when you were—"

"Flung to the ground? Yes."

He winced. "Part of it was an evaluation form your aunt put together for the brides to fill out after each wedding. There are some fifteen categories they're supposed to rate either *satisfactory* or *unsatisfactory*."

"You've got to be kidding me. Like what? Cake? Music? Favors?"

"Uh-huh. And organization, friendliness of staff, availability of the wedding planner ... Each category is worth a certain number of points and the final score determines whether the wedding was satisfactorily completed or not."

Delaney's mouth dropped open and she gaped at him for several speechless moments. "Give me a break. This job is just one delightful surprise after another," she bit out. "And what's the deal with those Henrys? They'll be the downfall of us all."

"They're the reason Dan and I wanted to hold the meetings," Mike lied, and quickly filled her in on the Henrys' history. "We don't want them to forget how many people are relying on them to complete their part. We're hoping that meeting every week will help them put aside their differences until this thing is over."

"Do you really think that's possible?"

He shrugged.

Delaney sighed and got up. "I'll be right back. I need a drink of water."

A minute later, the front-desk nurse was bending over him with a clipboard. "Mr. McBride, I need your wife to sign these papers, then we'll take her back to an exam room."

Mr. McBride? Disconcerted, Mike took the clipboard. "She's not—we're not—she's getting a drink."

"When she gets back, just have her sign where I put the red x's, then bring this up to the desk," the nurse said briskly before heading back toward the check-in station.

"Will do," Mike said to her back.

The nurse spotted Delaney returning to the waiting room and waved. "Mrs. McBride," she called, "I gave your husband some papers for you to sign. Then we're ready for you."

A confused expression flitted across Delaney's face and she stopped and threw a glance Mike's way and then looked back at the nurse.

"Just need your signature." The nurse gestured at Mike.

"Ohh, right." By the time Delaney reached Mike, she was grinning broadly. "Honey," she said, "you forgot my birthday again."

He found himself mesmerized by the sparkle in her hazel-green eyes. "Yeah? Well, you suck at remembering our anniversary."

She took the clipboard from him. "Obviously the bloom has gone off the rose."

Mike threw back his head and laughed. Pumpkin McBride was nobody's tagalong anymore.

4

———

Back at her apartment above Storybook Weddings, Delaney slouched into the worn sofa and flipped through *Money* magazine. Mike had been a good friend tonight, supportive, comfortable to be with. It felt good to be in this new place with him. "Those Henrys, on the other hand, are going to be trouble," she muttered.

As nice as each of the men might be individually, together they were like a screeching, out-of-tune duet. "All I have to say is, they'd better do their part. Much as I loved you, Aunt Ellie, I better not be going through wedding planning hell for nothing."

She pitched the magazine onto the glass-topped coffee table. The problem was, no one seemed to know how to get the Henrys to play nicely together. Not the executor. Not Dan. Not Mike.

She rubbed her wrist, now wrapped in a polyester brace with Velcro straps, her fingers sticking out the end like little sausages. Not broken, the doctor had said, just a sprain. She knew she should be happy about that, but even a sprain meant she would be one-handed for a couple of weeks.

She'd come to Birch Harbor determined to stay uninvolved. Yet, two days in town and already she'd jumped into the fray. If tonight's meeting was any indication, it was only going to get worse. She closed her eyes. She needed to talk to someone with more insight into the two Henrys than Mike, someone who'd known them for a good long time. And the only person she knew who fit that description was Ellie's brother, Great-Uncle Joe.

She scrubbed her hands over her face. She hadn't stopped in to see Joe yet because she'd never been close to him—not like she'd been with Ellie. As a kid, she'd always been a little afraid of him. He was a big man, physically imposing, and so serious all the time, so focused on making money, he never seemed to have any fun. He'd never even married.

Her mother said it was because his family lost everything during the depression and he grew up determined to never be poor again. All Delaney had known was that he spent nearly every minute working.

Still, she wasn't a kid anymore. And she doubted her uncle was the ogre she'd imagined him to be when she was young. After spending all his seventy years in Birch Harbor, Uncle Joe surely had some insight into the Henrys. Tomorrow she would pay him a visit and see what she could learn.

———

It was past nine when Mike stepped across the living room and followed the sound of music to where his eleven-year-old daughter, Andrea, was dancing in front of the full-length mirror at the end of the hall. She should be in bed by now. He hated having his mother babysit because she had no backbone as far as Andie was concerned. His daughter tossed her light brown hair and sang along with the song like she was on stage. When she spotted his reflection in the mirror, she spun round, glaring, her embarrassment at being caught evident in the pink of her cheeks.

She shut off the music. "Dad! What?"

"Where's Grandma?"

"In the basement doing wash."

No matter how often he told his mother not to, every time she came over she did the laundry. Said it made her feel useful. Drove him nuts.

"Homework done?" he asked.

Andie's expression grew defensive. "Almost."

His stomach tensed at the argument he knew lay ahead. "Andie, I thought we agreed that—"

"Dad, those teachers are *crazy*. They don't think we have lives other than school. I have a life! I have other things to do than homework. Why do they give us so much? And that Mr. Tory, he can't teach math. No one in the class knows what they're doing and—"

"This is just what happens when you get older. Responsibility increases and so does homework."

"I hate middle school."

He was beginning to hate it, too. Especially the melodrama.

"Only a couple more weeks and school's out for the summer. How much homework have you got left?"

"Some math problems. And I have to make a poster showing different types of energy. Do we have any poster board?"

"Is this thing due tomorrow?" He tried to keep the annoyance out of his voice.

"The day after."

"Andie! How long have you known about it? You know, if you get your work done first—" He stopped and exhaled. He'd given the same lecture fifty times this school year already and it never mattered. Obviously, he was saying something wrong, but he couldn't figure out what to change. He took her hand and gently pulled her toward the kitchen. "Come on, you need to finish and get to bed."

Her shoulders slumped as she plopped down at the kitchen table and opened her math book. Mike rubbed the back of his neck. If this was just the beginning of adolescence, he was in for trouble. He'd had custody of Andie since his divorce when she was a baby, and they'd always been close. But lately, it seemed, they were at odds as often as they got along. He wandered into the living room and picked up the purple ceramic dinosaur she had made him for Father's Day in the third grade.

"How's that new squash girl?" Andie called.

"Squash girl?"

"That one you knew when you were kids."

"You mean Pumpkin?"

"Yeah, her. What's she like?"

"Do your homework."

"I am!" Andie yelled. "So what's she like?"

Mike put the dinosaur down and went into the kitchen. He thought about seeing Pumpkin in the wedding shop and at the heirs' meeting, about taking her to the emergency room and their conversation there. "She's nice."

"Is she pretty?" Andie twirled her pencil.

Very pretty. "I guess so."

"Can't you tell?"

Andie's face registered disgust and he knew he sounded like a nerd. He could accept his daughter thinking that of him when she was sixteen, but he wasn't ready for it when she was just eleven. "Okay, she's pretty."

"*Really* pretty?'

"Yes, really pretty," he said, and Andie's eyes grew round. "Now do your homework."

Andie grinned.

"Who's really pretty?" His mother came up the basement steps with a laundry basket full of folded clothes.

"Pumpkin, the wedding planner," Andie said in a know-it-all voice.

"You're talking about Delaney McBride?" his mother asked.

"Yeah, Dad thinks she's gorgeous. Like a movie star. And he wants to go out with her."

Mike straightened. "Hey, wait a—"

"L-O-V-E," Andie spelled aloud.

"Michael, is this true?" His mother set the basket on the table and turned to face him.

"Yes." Andie laughed gleefully.

"No," Mike said. "Andie, knock it off."

"Michael, are you planning to go out with her?" His mother smiled.

"No." Except ... he was supposed to be romancing Pumpkin to make sure she stayed in town long enough to do all the weddings. "I mean, I don't know," he said, backtracking. "We just saw each other yesterday for the first time in years." He scowled at his daughter. "Don't go reading anything into this. If I do go out with Pumpkin while she's here, it'll just be because we're friends."

His mom picked up the laundry basket and headed down the hall. "I told you years ago to keep an eye on that one. I knew she would be a beauty someday."

———

Late the next morning, Delaney took a break from wedding planning and impulsively headed for the old bank building a few blocks away where Uncle Joe rented office space on the second floor. The sun was already warming the day and she felt like a tourist as she peered into the shop windows along the Main Street sidewalk. She inhaled the sweet smell of just-made fudge and let out a sigh; the fudge alone could be reason enough to stay here for two months.

The moment she opened the door to Joe's offices, she felt like she'd entered another world. The rich interior—dark woods, cordovan leather club chairs, thick Turkish carpet—was clearly the space of a man who enjoyed very nice things.

"I'm Delaney McBride," she said to the receptionist. "Joe Waverly is my uncle. I'm sorry I didn't call ahead, but is there any chance he has a few minutes?"

"Oh, Delaney!" The woman stood and shook Delaney's hand. "I'm Claire Hannoway. Joe figured he'd be hearing from you." She glanced at the phone on her desk and pointed at a steady red light. "He's been on a conference call for twenty minutes. I don't think it'll be too much longer. Why don't you have a seat and I'll let him know you're here. Would you like a cup of coffee or a water?"

"Water would be fine, thanks." As soon as Delaney settled into one of the club chairs, a brown and black pug raced down the hall toward her. The dog wiggled around at her feet, sniffing and snorting, and she reached down to pet his head. He licked her pants and she shifted her leg away.

Claire returned with a bottle of water. "That's your uncle's dog, Blue. Comes to the office every day."

Wasn't the name, Blue, reserved for hound dogs? Although this little pug did have soulful eyes like a hound. Delaney opened the water and took a sip.

"So you've taken over Storybook Weddings," Claire said. "How do you like it?"

"Not so bad, I guess. But it's only day three."

"Ellie was renowned for her weddings." Claire returned to her desk.

"So I hear." Delaney felt something odd against her calf and looked down to find the dog humping her leg. She pushed him gently away with one hand. "I'll just do the best I can, learning on the job. Wedding planning isn't exactly something you study in school."

"How about the other heirs? How are they doing with their tasks?" Claire filed some papers in the cabinet behind her desk.

"Well ... we've all agreed we're in this together. We succeed as a group." A picture of the Henrys fist fighting flashed through her mind. Yeah, they'd succeed all right—at killing one another.

"Ellie's will was all the talk when it first got read, what with those stipulations. It was nice of your aunt to remember the Henrys and Mike and Dan. And you, of course. I think everyone was surprised she left Joe out of the will, but then, maybe she thought he didn't need the money."

He *didn't* need the money.

From the hallway came a deep voice. "But I am in the will. If the heirs fail, I get everything whether I need it or not."

Delaney turned to see her great-uncle, still a bear of a man, coming toward her, grinning. Suddenly she realized he wasn't a grizzly, he was a teddy. Why had she been so afraid of him as a kid? She stood to give him a hug.

"I'm glad you stopped by. Come on back. What'd you do to your wrist?"

"Just a sprain." Delaney followed him to his office, and they settled in leather chairs at a glass coffee table. "I'm so sorry about Aunt Ellie. Somehow, I always thought she'd live forever."

"We all did. It was a shock. Three months after the diagnosis, she was gone." His pain was palpable.

"I didn't even know she was sick." Tears sprang to her eyes and she blinked them away.

"She didn't want anyone to know. Called it an *inconvenience* that wasn't worth bothering people with. Said there were far more interesting things to be concerned about than an old woman's health."

"That sounds like her."

Silence settled over them for a moment. Then Joe asked, "How's the wedding planning? Everything going all right?"

"Wedding planning is going okay. It's the rest of the will that I'm worried about. That's why I'm here—to get some advice." She held up her braced wrist and began to describe last night's meeting.

It took only a few minutes for her uncle to confirm what she'd suspected. Stonewall was a worrier; he fretted even when things were going well. Sully, on the other hand, was an optimist.

"And Henry Clark was a pragmatist," her uncle said. "He'd sit down with the two of them over a bottle of Jameson and pretty soon they'd all be in agreement. Finest Irish whiskey there is, he used to say." Joe smiled. "Not sure whether that'll be much help to you."

Delaney laughed. "Me either. But I'll pick up a bottle and keep it on hand in case I get desperate."

"You get desperate about anything and you let me know. I'll do whatever I can to help," he said. "I want all of you to succeed because that's what Ellie wanted."

Delaney cocked her head. "As long as you mention it, what *did* she want? I'm still trying to figure out why she wrote a will like this."

"Just eccentric, I guess. You know how some people get. I think it was her way of making one last connection with the people she loved."

Delaney was tempted to say that a conventional will without contingencies would have been an even nicer connection, but decided against it.

By the time she headed back to Storybook Weddings

half an hour later, she was more determined than ever to fulfill her aunt's last wishes. If Jameson was what it took to keep the Henrys in line, she'd buy a bottle a week. Striding down the sidewalk, she passed Hobart & Hobart Auto Repair and Service Station and spotted Dan talking to a customer at the gas pump.

He waved her over. "How's the wrist?"

"Better."

"You want to see your aunt's old Chevy? It's in the fourth bay." He pointed into the garage at a red car with white tail fins and yelled, "Hey, Mike, someone to see you!"

Mike was here? "Oh, well, I probably shouldn't—"

"Just go on in."

"Thanks." *Just great.* He'd probably think she was stalking him. She stepped carefully across the stained concrete floor, reaching the Chevy just as Mike rolled out from underneath, flat on his back on a creeper.

He grinned up at her, then got to his feet. "Hey, there."

"Isn't it easier to work on the car when it's up in the air?"

"We don't have a lift in the fourth bay." Mike pulled a rag from the back pocket of his jeans to wipe off his hands. Then he absently brushed off the seat of his pants. "How's your wrist this morning?"

"Better already."

"Good. I feel guilty enough for insisting you come to that meeting last night. What can I do for you?"

She took in his messy brown hair and his blue eyes and his open smile and his well-worn jeans slung low on his hips and his shirt coming untucked ... and then she reminded herself of what good friends they were becoming. "I-I was just passing by. Went to see if my uncle had any advice about the Henrys. And then I saw Dan out in front and he waved me over and asked if I wanted to see the car and so here I am."

Why did the truth suddenly sound like a lie? She eyed the Chevy so she could avoid looking at Mike. "Shouldn't you be filing legal briefs or something?"

"That's on the docket for this afternoon. Dan and I wanted to check out a few things on the car, so I came in here first. Did your uncle have any brilliant ideas?"

"Jameson."

"Whiskey?"

She nodded. "Finest Irish whiskey there is."

"Well, if it works, count me in. Maybe I should pick up a bottle before the next heirs' meeting. If that doesn't get the Henrys together, then at least the rest of us can drown our sorrows."

Delaney laughed and looked at the car again. "So this is Uncle Henry's Chevy. I hardly remember him driving it."

"That's because it was already twenty years old when you were born. Your aunt said he kept it because it was the car he courted her in."

Another hopeless romantic—he and Ellie had been a perfect match. "Will it be hard to fix?"

"For hardly being driven in the past fifteen years, it's not bad. Needs brakes. Some bodywork. Mice nested in the backseat, so we've got to pull the seat out for reupholstering. The tires are rotted. About what you'd expect."

"About what *you'd* expect. I, on the other hand, would have no clue. Here's what I know about cars—they're red or blue or gold or black—"

"I'd be happy to teach you."

"How to fix cars?

"It's fun. You might like it."

She laughed. "I have enough to learn right now about wedding planning. And if I don't get back to the shop pretty soon, I'm going to fail at that." Mike was so wrong. Fixing cars with him wouldn't be fun, it'd be torture. She'd have to see him pull a rag out of his back pocket and not let herself notice how well his jeans fit. She'd have to watch him tighten lug nuts on a wheel and not let herself notice the muscles in his arms. She'd have to listen to what he was teaching her and not let herself notice what a really nice guy he was.

She couldn't notice Mike. Not now, not ever. Because if she let herself notice, then she would want him. And that was just plain stupid. She didn't need to tangle up her life like that, didn't need to experience one more short-term relationship destined to go nowhere.

Seriously? Fix cars with Mike Connery? Not on her life.

5

Delaney scowled at the bolts of silver and white netting on the worktable in the back room of Storybook Weddings and had the sudden urge to bite her nails even though she'd broken herself of the habit years ago.

She had to cut three hundred five-inch squares out of this netting. Then she had to set five silver and pearl-colored, chocolate-filled after-dinner mints on each square, fold up the sides and tie a silver ribbon around each one. And from each ribbon, she had to hang a tiny silver ring as a symbol of unbroken love.

By the time she finished this project, she suspected those rings would symbolize unbroken insanity. *Hers.* She had to make a mere three hundred mint packages before Saturday's wedding. Never mind all the other details she had to get done.

All this with a sprained wrist. Thank goodness Lauren would be able to help out tomorrow.

But once Lauren had the baby, Delaney wasn't sure who she could call on. Her stomach turned, and she tamped down her panic. Sometimes it was better not to think of things until absolutely necessary.

With a sigh, she picked up the scissors and began to cut out squares. Silver, white, silver, white, silver ... "Someone please shoot me now," she muttered. "Six feet under would be preferable to slow death by boredom." Silver, white ...

A scraping sound drew her attention, and she raised her head to see a young girl in shorts and a T-shirt watching her from the workroom doorway, a backpack slung over one shoulder, her long hair straggling loose from its ponytail. The girl rubbed a sneakered foot against the floor.

How did this kid get all the way across the shop without making a sound? Wasn't that bell supposed to jangle whenever the entrance door opened? "Hi," Delaney said. "Can I help you with something?"

The girl shrugged. "What did you mean, that thing about six feet under?"

"Oh, that ... that was about six feet of netting I have to put under the ... wedding cake for decoration," she said, trying to sound believable. "I talk to myself all the time. I didn't hear you come in. The bell didn't jingle."

"I opened the door really carefully so it wouldn't."

"And why is that?"

"I just wanted to see what you looked like."

"Oh. I'm Delaney McBride. Do I look okay?"

The girl nodded. "I already know who you are. I'm Andrea Connery, but everyone calls me Andie."

Delaney eyed Andie thoughtfully. "Are you related to Mike?"

"He's my dad."

"Your dad?" Mike had a child? Did he have a wife, too?

She kept her voice casual. "We go back a long time. I've known him since I was five."

"He said you were pretty."

Delaney's cheeks warmed. So did her heart. "That was nice of him."

Andie studied herself in the mirror on a nearby wall. "I hope I'm pretty someday."

"You're pretty now."

Andie snorted. "I know what I look like. And I don't look like the popular girls."

Delaney felt a wave of recognition. This girl was not a blue-eyed blonde, lithe and physically mature beyond her years. "No, you don't. But you know what? Neither did I. And I guess I turned out okay, huh? I mean, your dad said I was pretty." She continued cutting squares of netting.

"What are you making?"

"Favors for the wedding guests to take home."

"Or eat."

"Or eat. I need to make three hundred of these things," Delaney said.

Andie let her backpack slide off her shoulder to the floor. "My dad told me you hurt your wrist. I could help you."

Delaney lifted her head, ready to decline the offer, but the sight of Mike's blue eyes in the child's face changed her mind. "How old are you?"

"Eleven. I used to help your aunt sometimes. She would have me do stuff for the weddings."

Delaney handed her the scissors. "Well, then, I guess you could help me, too."

"She paid me five dollars an hour."

Ah. A shrewd businesswoman. She'd have liked this kid whether Mike was her father or not. "Of course. That's only fair."

"She called me when she needed help. Or I would stop by after school and see." Andie bent over the netting and got busy.

"Then, that's what we'll do."

The two worked in silence for several minutes. Then Andie asked, "Were you surprised to be in the will?"

"Uh, yeah," Delaney said, taken aback. "I live on the East Coast, so I've only seen my great-aunt a few times since we moved out of town. The will was a shock." *Shock* was an understatement.

"It was a shock around here, too."

She could understand that. At least whatever gossip was about her didn't involve sending love notes to Mike Connery this time.

"Everyone thought she'd leave her money to her brother."

"She probably figured he had enough of his own."

"Maybe." Andie stopped cutting to count her netting squares. "But Claire, his girlfriend—"

"Claire's his girlfriend?"

"Uh-huh. My friend Emma says her mom calls it a *working relationship*. Anyway, Emma's mom said Claire said the money should have stayed in Ellie's family, or something like that."

"I *am* in the family," Delaney said. "Ellie was my great-aunt."

Andie cocked her head. "I bet Claire forgot about that."

An hour later, she and Andie had made real forward

progress, both with the favors and with the latest gossip around town. In the midst of pattering on about one person or another, Andie offered up that she'd been born in Chicago, and her parents divorced when she was two.

"I'm sorry," Delaney said. "Does your mom live in town?"

"No. She lives in Berlin. She's an international lawyer. I don't see her very often."

Delaney searched for something to say that didn't sound either pitying or cavalier. "That must be hard sometimes."

Andie shrugged. "I'm used to it."

Used to not seeing her mother? She didn't doubt that was true, but suspected there was some bravado talking here, too.

"My other grandma lives in Ohio. I hardly ever see her, either. That's why I like it here." Andie gestured with the scissors. "Because my grandma and grandpa are here. And my Auntie Jane comes over all the time because she's only an hour away. She's married and going to have a baby, so then I'll have a cousin."

"Congratulations."

"I hope she still comes to visit as much when the baby is born," Andie said in a low voice.

Delaney raised her head, hearing in Andie's tone the young girl's longing for a mother. "Oh, I'm sure she will."

"Auntie Jane says I have my finger on the pulse of Birch Harbor."

Auntie Jane might be right about that. Delaney dropped some mints on the netting square, pulled the four corners to center, slid a silver ring on the ribbon and tied a bow around the little package.

"What does she mean?" Andie looked at her innocently. "My finger on the pulse of Birch Harbor?"

Delaney swallowed a laugh. "It means you know what's going on."

"Oh. That's what my grandma says, too."

The bell at the front door jangled, and Delaney slipped off her stool and went out into the shop. Late-afternoon sun streamed through the picture windows and sparkled on the tiara display. Mike, smiling and dressed in a dark suit and starched white shirt, moved toward her. Quite a change from the dirty jeans and T-shirt he'd been wearing this morning.

"Well, hello. I see you've taken on your attorney persona this afternoon," she said.

"Had to go to court. Hey, I wanted to give you a heads-up. My daughter used to help Ellie out around here. She may come by to—"

"She's here. Helping me make favors."

Mike frowned. "Are you kidding? Any excuse to not do homework. Is she in the back?"

Delaney nodded and headed toward the workroom with Mike on her heels. "Hey, Andie, look who I found in the shop."

When she spotted Mike, the girl's face fell. She set the scissors on a pile of netting squares. "Oh. Dad."

Mike stopped in the doorway. "Andie, what are you doing here?"

"She hired me." Andie slid off her stool.

"What about that energy poster you have to make? And the rest of your homework?"

"I can do it later." Andie tossed her ponytail. "How's

she supposed to do all this stuff by herself with a wrecked wrist?"

"Andrea ..." Mike's voice held a tone of warning.

The tension between the two was unmistakable, and Delaney wondered whether Mike fully realized the impact his ex-wife's absence was having on his daughter. "Andie's been a big help today. I'd be way behind if she hadn't stopped by." She put a hand on Andie's shoulder. "But, Andie, your dad is right. Your main job has to be school. So if you're going to keep working for me—and I hope you do— you have to finish your homework first. Okay?"

Andie stared at her like she was a traitor.

"I'm going to need your help around here to get everything done. Deal?" Delaney held her breath.

Andie huffed and picked up her backpack where she'd dropped it. "Okay."

"Good," Delaney said. "See you tomorrow."

When Andie was out the door, Mike shook his head. "Something's wrong and I can't figure out what it is. One minute she's the same sweet kid she's always been. And the next she's moody and hates school and me."

"She's a teenager."

"She's *eleven*," Mike said.

"Eleven is the new thirteen."

"If you're right, it's going to be a long road."

Delaney walked with him toward the front door. She didn't want to make him worry over something he couldn't change, but if she was right about Andie, he should know what he was dealing with. "It might have something to do with her mother being gone."

"She told you about her mother?" He looked stunned.

"Not a lot."

He shook his head. "Not much I can do about it. She took a job in Berlin almost four years ago—international trade attorney for a multinational firm. A great job if that's your primary goal, but it means Andie's only contact with her mother is an occasional visit or phone call, and presents on her birthday and Christmas."

"I'm sorry." Delaney felt a wave of empathy for Mike's daughter.

"Just the cards we've been dealt." He nodded toward the workroom. "Thanks for what you said back there. That was the least resistance I've seen her put up over homework in the past six months." He opened the door and stepped outside, then stuck his head back in. "So, ah, you want to go out for a drink sometime?"

A moment passed before she found her voice. "Sure."

"Da-ad! I have homework to do!" Andie yelled from the street.

He rolled his eyes. "I'll talk to you later."

Delaney grinned after him like the village idiot. Was it possible that Mike Connery was actually beginning to see her as someone other than Pumpkin McBride, the gnat?

Head under the hood of a Taurus in the first bay of Hobart's Garage, Dan glanced at Mike, standing next to the car. "Has Pumpkin said anything about staying to do all five weddings yet?"

"She's only been here a few days. Give her some time."

"We don't have time. You need to kick the romance

program into gear." Dan reached for the wrench he'd set off to one side, patting his hand around in frustration when it didn't appear under his fingers. "Which, I might add, shouldn't exactly be torturous with the way Pumpkin looks now."

Dan was right about that. They'd always known Pumpkin was smart, but who would have guessed she'd turn out beautiful? Who, besides his mother, that was. He picked up the wrench and handed it to Dan. "Way ahead of you. I asked her out for a drink."

"Good man." Dan straightened. "Once Pumpkin has the money in hand, she'll probably thank you for getting her to stay."

"Yeah." He felt a twinge of guilt and pushed it away. As long as he kept things between them in control, as long as Pumpkin never figured out that his interest in her was driven by the will, everything would be fine.

6

———

DELANEY SAT ACROSS THE TABLE FROM THE BRIDE AND the mother of the bride for the upcoming weekend wedding. The young twenty-something was in a panic.

A groundless panic, Delaney thought. Because as far as this girl and her mother knew, everything was in place for the perfect event; they had no inkling that the wedding soloist had canceled this morning because of severe laryngitis. Nor did they know that every other singer Delaney had called was already booked for Saturday. No, this bride was creating drama simply because that was what she did. Because she was from a moderately well-to-do family, a spoiled princess with streaked golden hair.

"Mother, it's my *wedding.* I'm only getting married once, and I want everything to be perfect," the bride said in a demanding voice. She lay an accusing look on Delaney. "No one told us that Mrs. Clark passed on and you were taking over."

The mother patted her daughter's hand. "Honey, I'm sure Miss McBride knows what she's doing."

"Absolutely." Delaney wished she were at the end of this meeting instead of the beginning. "My aunt was very thorough. There's not much I need to do." Well, okay, there was plenty she needed to do, but why distress the bride any further? "In fact, my aunt was so well organized, I should probably stay out of the way and let things run themselves!" She gave them her best I'm-on-your-side smile.

Neither woman smiled back.

"Of course, I mean that only in the rhetorical sense."

"Is the white carriage ready?" The bride began to gnaw at the cuticle on her index finger, then jerked her hand away as if suddenly realizing her nails would be less than flawless on her wedding day. "The little bags of pearl and silver mints? The tiered cake with seashells and starfish cascading down the side? And the DJ? Does he know he's supposed to play *Under the Sea* when we arrive?"

The DJ! A trickle of sweat ran down the center of Delaney's back. She hadn't confirmed with him yet. She forced her lips to stay curved in a smile and dug deep into her limited wedding vocabulary. "Everything is set. Saturday will be a lovely beginning to your life of wedded bliss. There's just ... one small detail that came up this morning. Your soprano soloist called and it seems she has laryngitis."

"I knew it!" The bride's voice quavered. "I knew that my perfect wedding—"

"Does that mean she can't sing at all?" the mother asked.

Delaney blinked. *She can if you think croaking is singing.* "She can hardly talk. You know, I'd like to think of this as an opportunity to make the wedding even more perfect."

The bride gaped at her and Delaney kept talking. "I know several other excellent singers, so this will be a nonissue in no time. For now, though—" she said, standing, "—the favors are finished, so let me show them to you."

By the time she got the two women out of the shop, Delaney felt like she'd run a marathon. It had taken everything she had to keep the bride calm. Now all she had to do was call the DJ and find a singer.

Nothing to it.

She couldn't wait to have this first wedding over with.

And the second and the third and the fourth ...

Actually, she wished she could chuck it all and go back to her life in advertising where she felt competent, together, and in control. Too bad she had no life in advertising to go back to.

If only Nora's connection in San Francisco had offered her a job, she wouldn't be in the middle of this mess. Maybe one of her other cousins—Liza in Chicago or Izzy in St. Louis—knew someone in advertising who would want to hire—

Arghhh. Maybe she should stay focused on finding a singer. In desperation, she dialed the DJ scheduled for Saturday, The Incomparable Bobby C, and crossed her fingers that he could help.

By the time he finally answered—on the seventh ring— she was ready to jump through the phone. "I'm so glad you're there! I'm handling the weddings for my late aunt, who owned Storybook Weddings, and I'm just following up to make sure you're—"

"Doing the wedding this weekend?" he asked. "All set. Ocean theme. Beach songs. Let's see … *Under the Sea* when the couple arrives. The bridal dance is *Hawaiian Wedding Song*. The parents' dance is *Beyond the Sea*. Make sure I play the Beach Boys, some reggae, and lots of fun dance music."

Delaney felt her tension begin to ease. "Thank you! It's such a relief to know I don't have to worry about the reception music."

He laughed. "You shouldn't have to worry about any of the suppliers. Ellie Clark was like a general—we were her troops. She was such a perfectionist about her weddings, nobody ever got out of line because they knew she'd replace them in a heartbeat. I'm going to miss her."

"I think a lot of people will," Delaney said. "I could sure use one of her replacements right now." She explained the problem with the soloist. "If you have any thoughts, I'm all ears."

Silence.

"Bobby C?" she prodded.

"Yeah. Jeez, I don't know. I could play a recording if you want. No flat notes guaranteed."

"Thanks, but I don't think that will cut it. See you Saturday." Delaney hung up the phone, slumped back into the wooden desk chair and closed her eyes. Would the bride give her low ratings on the wedding-evaluation form because the soloist got laryngitis? How many points could she lose before a wedding was deemed *unsatisfactory*?

For the second time in half an hour, she longed for her old job at the ad agency and her nice, neat desk and its ergonomic chair that hugged and supported her as she worked.

"Hey, Delaney, do you need me to work today?"

She jerked upright and looked directly at Andie, just two feet away. "You're going to give me a heart attack. How do you get in that door without making the bell jingle?"

Andie laughed as though proud of herself. She dropped her backpack on the floor.

Delaney shook her head. "Homework before anything else."

"Awww—"

"Get your books out. I'm not getting in trouble with your dad." She watched Andie unzip her backpack and set some paper and a couple of books on the work table. "You don't happen to know any singers, do you?" she asked in desperation. "The soloist for Saturday's wedding has laryngitis."

Andie climbed onto one of the stools. "You could ask my dad. He was in the band in high school."

"He played trumpet, Honey. He wasn't a singer."

"He can sing, too."

"We all can—in the shower." Delaney shook her head.

"He's pretty smart. Maybe he'll have an idea."

"Unless he's got a singer tucked away somewhere, all the good ideas in the world aren't going to help me."

Andie shrugged. "What else are you going to do?"

Leave it to a kid to cut to the chase. "Well, I ..." What *was* she going to do? "When does your dad get home from work?"

"He plays baseball for Ollie's Tap every Wednesday.

Afterward he goes to the bar and my grandma stays with me. You could go to the game tonight."

Mike was still playing baseball? Back in high school, she used to sit in the bleachers and fantasize that when he waved at the fans in the stands, he was waving at her. Watching him play had been the high point of her summer nights. She smiled to herself. It would be fun to see him on the field again. Besides, he *had* asked her about going for a drink.

"I suppose it wouldn't hurt to ask your dad about a singer. Maybe I'll be lucky and he'll actually know someone I can call." She stood and went over to the work table. "So ... what time is the game?"

———

Delaney sat in her BMW in Ollie's parking lot but made no move to go into the bar. A breeze slipped through the open windows, soft, like cotton sheets on naked skin when the heat of the day has lingered well beyond darkness. It was the kind of night for falling in love.

She thought of Drew, the man she'd dated for two years —until he decided that what he wanted to be was friends with benefits. And before him, Will, who got so settled in their relationship it ceased being a relationship. And before him, Christopher, who broke up with her and married some woman he'd only known for three weeks. And a host of other dates that only served to reinforce what she'd learned at her mother's knee. There was only one person you could rely on in this world: yourself.

But every now and then, usually on nights like this

when the sky was full of stars and the summer was in the air and all of life seemed flush with promise, she wished she had gotten it all wrong, that love could start and not end, that there really was such a thing as a happy ending.

And then, after a few moments of yearning, she would be smart enough to put that thought completely out of her mind.

A couple of players wearing pinstriped jerseys with the name *Ollie's* stitched across the back crossed the lot. Their obviously high spirits had to mean they'd won their game. As the men pulled open the door to the bar, music from the jukebox escaped into the night, then was quickly recaptured as the door swung shut.

She hadn't gone to the game after all. Had spent so long vacillating about whether or not to go—and what Mike would think if she did—that she finally decided to just show up at the bar once the game was over. So here she was.

In the parking lot.

She peered at the tavern sign shining in the darkness, at the blinking neon signs illuminating the windows. Mike was inside that building. Mike Connery, her first infatuation. She almost wished he hadn't mentioned going out for a drink yesterday because she didn't want him to think she was using the soloist problem as an excuse to chase him down in the bar. After all, she could have just as easily asked for his help by phone.

Well, if he read anything into her coming here tonight, that was *his* problem. Because she wasn't infatuated with him anymore. No way. And as soon as all the weddings were finished, she would be headed back to Boston, chasing down the future she'd put on hold to come here.

She shoved open her car door and stepped out.

———

Mike toasted the team's win with Dan, then leaned his elbows on the bar and took a big swallow of his beer. "I'm still trying to figure out why Ellie wrote this will. If she wanted us to have the car, why didn't she just give it to us?"

"Maybe she wanted to make sure we'd bring it back to its former glory," Dan said over the music.

"She had to realize we would have fixed it up no matter what."

Dan shrugged. "Well, none of it makes sense. Look at the Henrys. The only thing they get when all is said and done is the satisfaction that the city has a new band shell."

"They do get the chance to work together." Mike grinned.

Dan finished off his beer and pushed the glass toward the bartender for a refill. "Yeah, that's going to be pleasant for everyone involved."

"Hey, check it out." Mike nodded at a table in the dining area across the bar where Sully and his wife were having burgers with Pumpkin's great-uncle, Joe. Mike waved. "All we need is Stonewall and Pumpkin and we could hold an heirs' meeting."

"What do you think Ellie was trying to do with Pumpy? Making someone come here for two months is pretty demanding when they have another job," Dan said.

"Maybe Ellie wanted to force her to make a tough decision."

Dan played with the coaster on the bar. "Like what?"

"Her job versus her inheritance. Her high-powered life versus the excitement of Birch Harbor. I don't know. I'm just talking. I have no idea." Mike took another swallow of his beer.

"So how many days until you start setting the hook?" Dan swiveled on his bar stool and surveyed the crowded bar.

Mike frowned. "What hook?"

"Pumpkin. When are you having that drink?"

"Oh, yeah. She's too busy until this wedding is over."

"Don't wait too long. We can't risk her throwing in the towel." Dan glanced at the front door, then slid off his bar stool. "There's Lauren."

Mike watched as Dan sneaked up behind his wife and planted a kiss on the back of her neck. She started, then twisted round to kiss him full on the mouth.

He felt a sudden wistfulness and turned away, his thoughts on the woman he'd once loved, the woman his love couldn't keep. Cassie had been pregnant with Andie when they married, and he'd foolishly thought the baby would make them a family, tied to one another by love. But before two years were out, Cassie had left him and Andie, determined to make her way to the top of the legal profession.

Dan appeared at his side and leaned toward him. "Don't look now, but you've just been handed the opportunity of a lifetime."

Mike shifted his gaze to the bar's entranceway. Pumpkin stood just inside the door seeming more than a little lost.

"Looks to me like she needs a friend," Dan said under his breath.

Without another word or a sideways glance, Mike got up and began to work his way toward her through the crowd.

7

———

"Can I get you a drink?"

Delaney turned toward the voice. *Mike.* In his short-sleeved jersey, it was obvious he still had the physique of an athlete. Her heart skipped a beat, a reaction that had to be little more than muscle memory. "Uh, sure. How about a Diet Coke?"

He raised his brows. "We won tonight. And you're having a Diet Coke?" The sparkle in his blue eyes began to make her melt, just like when she was a kid. Old habits certainly died hard. "When in Rome ..." he said.

God, he was cute. She laughed, "All right. Make it a rum and Diet Coke." If he couldn't help her with the name of a soloist, her mind might need a little numbing before this night was over.

"That's better. Come on." He led her to where Lauren and Dan were sitting at the bar. "Anyone want anything?"

"I'll have another water," Lauren said as Dan held up his nearly full beer bottle and shook his head.

Mike moved to an empty spot at the bar and waved at the bartender.

"How's the wedding planning coming along?" Dan asked Delaney over the din.

She frowned. "Not so good at the moment. The soloist canceled—she's got laryngitis."

Lauren gasped. "I was working today. When did this happen?"

"About an hour after you left. I would have called, but I knew you had a doctor's appointment." She shook her head. "I called every singer on my aunt's list. They're all booked. I've got about one day to fix this before our inheritances collapse like a reception tent in a tornado."

"It might not mean the end," Lauren said. "A wedding is about love and commitment, not about who sings the songs."

"Nice sentiment, but I'm not sure this bride and you are of the same opinion," Delaney said. "For her, it's more about the soloist and the flowers. And the white carriage and the seashells on her cake. And woe to the wedding planner who doesn't deliver."

"Doesn't deliver what?" Mike handed her a tumbler of rum and Diet Coke.

"Doesn't deliver the fairytale wedding she's expecting." Delaney used the skinny red straw to stab at the lime wedge floating in her drink.

Mike looked from Delaney to Lauren to Dan. "Am I missing something?"

Delaney took a sip of her drink and savored the taste. Then she took another, larger sip. "Here's the thing. It's the soloist." She proceeded to fill Mike in on her current disaster. "So my question is. Actually it's *questions*, plural.

First do you know where I can get a soloist on short notice? And second, if we end up without a singer at the wedding and the bride gives me a zero in the music category on the evaluation form, will it lower my score enough to mean the whole gig is up?"

Mike set his hands on the bar and leaned forward as he considered the question.

"Hmm," Dan said. "If a wedding takes place in the woods and there isn't anyone to hear the music, is there really a wedding?"

"Drink your beer and shut up," Mike said. "I don't think a bad score in one category would doom you. But there's a bigger, more ominous question. What if the bride gets so upset about the missing soloist that she marks you down in several categories?"

"As long as the vows are exchanged, I'd call it a successful wedding." Dan put his arm around his wife. "Wouldn't you, hon?"

Lauren nodded. "But it's not what we think that matters."

"Exactly. And like I said before, this particular bride might disagree with all of us about what constitutes success." Delaney couldn't keep the discouragement out of her voice.

"I guess that's why your aunt created that form. To make the process less subjective," Mike said.

"Except for on the part of the bride," Lauren pointed out.

"This speculation isn't helping me find a soloist, which would be the first step to saving our overall score for this wedding. Don't you guys know anyone who can sing? At this point I'm not asking for a fantastic voice, just one good enough to carry a tune. I can always have the pianist play louder to hide any flat notes." She turned to Lauren.

"Don't look at me!" Lauren said. "If I sing, I'll empty the church. But, Mike, how about—"

"No."

"No, who?" Delaney asked.

"Why not?" Lauren grinned.

"Who? And why not?" Delaney pressed. "Come on, Mike, I'm at my wit's end here. All choices have to be brought forward and I'll eliminate them once I know what they are."

"She's right," Dan said. "Might be the only shot we have."

"Who?" Delaney raised her eyebrows.

Mike grimaced. "Me."

"You? Andie said the same thing. You mean you can actually sing?"

"Like a nightingale." Lauren let out an appreciative laugh.

"Only lower," Dan added.

"This is a joke, right?"

Dan and Lauren shook their heads.

"When did this happen?" Delaney asked, incredulous. She felt a flicker of hope.

Mike shrugged. "I started growing into it my senior year."

"By college, he could've been in a boy band." Dan did an upper-body dance move on his bar stool.

Mike snorted.

Delaney looked at Lauren. "Does he sing well enough to do a wedding?"

"The boy could have a nice side business if he wanted one."

"Okay, then," Delaney said to Mike. "You're hired. I'll get you the songs. You'll have two days to practice."

"Wait a minute—"

"You have a better idea?"

He opened his mouth, then closed it without saying a word.

"That's what I thought. Don't worry. There's only four songs."

"Four? When am I going to learn them?"

"Relax. They're all standard wedding fare. You probably already know every one. I'll drop off the sheet music in the morning." Delaney took another sip of her drink. "Can you read music?"

"Well enough."

"It's okay if you can't. Old Mrs. Keely, the pianist, said she'd practice with whoever I found to sing." She smiled brightly at Mike so he wouldn't have the heart to change his mind.

"I think it's only appropriate that we celebrate Mike's foray into his new singing career with another beverage," Dan said. He raised a hand for the bartender and placed an order just as Sully approached them with Delaney's uncle.

"You kids seem awfully serious for having just won a ball game," Sully said to Mike. He turned to Delaney. "How's your wrist?"

"I don't have time to think about it," she said. "I'm

already onto new problems. The soloist for Saturday's wedding canceled—laryngitis."

Joe's mouth dropped open. "What'll you do?"

"Mike's going to sing."

Sully put a hand on Mike's shoulder. "Didn't know you had the music in you."

"Well, it remains to be seen," Mike said wryly.

"He's the best I've got," Delaney said.

The bartender returned with two beers, a rum and Diet Coke, and a water. "You gentlemen want something?" Dan asked.

"I could be persuaded," Sully said.

"Not for me, thanks," Joe said. "Just wanted to say hi on my way out."

Two hours later, Delaney was still at the tavern, sipping her fourth rum and Diet Coke and thinking how glad she was that her apartment was within walking distance. She'd come back in the morning to pick up her car. She leaned against a support pillar and watched Mike and Dan finish a wobbly game of pool.

"Six ball in the side pocket." She pointed with her drink. The ad agency where she'd worked had a pool table in the lounge. They had a TV, too, but on breaks, everyone played pool.

Mike bent over the table, index finger of his left hand crooked over the stick to guide his shot. He squinted up at her. "You know how to play?"

"A little. Up for another game?"

He dropped the ball in the pocket. After a few more shots, he put the game away, then sidled over to Delaney. "Think you can play with that wrist of yours?"

She saw the challenge in his eyes and met it with her own. "Rack 'em. What's the forfeit?"

He looked at her in surprise, then became thoughtful, as though considering a number of options.

"How about a kiss?" Lauren offered.

Delaney, Dan, and Mike all turned to her at once.

Delaney shook her head. "Oh, no."

"Now that's a novel bet. I like it. Mike?" Dan's expression was all mischief.

Mike's gaze met Delaney's. In the darkness of the bar, his eyes were no longer blue. They were black—dangerous black. He nodded slowly. "Yeah, okay, a kiss. When I win, you have to kiss me."

"On the lips," Dan added.

She rolled her eyes. Kissing Mike was out of the question. Her knees would probably give out and she'd end up on the floor, somehow transformed into the same blithering, infatuated teenager she'd been fifteen years ago. She could, on the other hand, avoid the whole problem by winning—which shouldn't be a problem because she'd had some great teachers at the agency. She grinned. "Okay. You're on."

Dan waved his beer bottle in their direction. "And if Delaney wins, Mike has to kiss her."

She tightened her grip on her glass. "No, no, no. Each person names their own forfeit. If I win, Mike has to ..." She searched her brain for something more appropriate.

"Has to wash and wax Delaney's car," Lauren said. She tossed a wicked grin Delaney's way, then placed her attention squarely on Mike. "Shirtless. Barefoot. And in running shorts—those short, navy-blue ones with the rip on the right leg." She leaned over to whisper in Delaney's ear, "Have you ever seen him without a shirt on?" She fanned herself.

Just the thought made Delaney faint enough. The real thing would probably do her in.

"Okay, we have an agreement. A kiss on the lips for a car wash almost in the buff," Dan said. "*Rack 'em up.*"

"You break," Mike said.

Heart pounding, she set her drink on a nearby table, chose a cue stick, and chalked the end.

"Need any tips?" Mike took a swallow of beer.

"I think I'll be okay." She rested the cue across the brace on her wrist and took aim, concentrating to clear the effects of the rum from her head, if that was even possible. Then she made the opening break, neatly pocketing the nine and leaving the cue ball centered on the table—in perfect position to make a couple more shots.

Mike looked at her, impressed. "Somehow, I'm thinking you've played more than a little."

"Somehow, I think you're right." She sent another two balls into pockets.

Dan let out a whoop. "Mikey, you may have just met your match."

She missed her next shot and threw a humorous glare at Dan. "Your turn, Mike."

He stepped around the table, studying his options. Delaney watched his hands as he chalked his cue—strong hands. She wondered what it would feel like to have one of those hands wrapped around one of hers. To have both of those hands touching her.

Mike deftly sent the three ball into the corner pocket

and she jerked her attention back to the game. He dropped another ball in before missing the next shot. A couple of guys from the neighboring pool table stopped playing to watch the game. Within minutes, word of their bet had spread throughout the bar and a large audience had gathered.

Delaney raised her chin and gestured with her stick. "Ten ball in the side pocket," she said with smug confidence.

He smiled as though he knew better. She lined up to shoot and promptly missed. A groan went up among the spectators. Damn, he *did* know better.

Mike gave her a smirk, then began to methodically clear the table. One ball after another dropped into a pocket. For the first time in the game, she began to feel the heat. Working at the agency, she'd gotten pretty good at pool— and she liked to win.

Scratch that. She hated to lose.

At anything.

Now he had only one ball left to play before the eight. Her heart began to pound; this absolutely could not be happening. She was going to lose to Mike? And have to kiss him in front of all these people? Sweat prickled across her shoulders. She stared at the table, willing him to miss his last shot, even as the teenage girl she'd once been irrationally hoped that he would make it.

He chalked his cue, then bent to the table. The room hushed until the only sound was that of the jukebox playing, "Money." Then he drove the final ball into the corner pocket and took aim at the eight.

Miss, miss, miss, she willed the ball.

As if taunting her, the round black traitor dropped into the pocket

A cheer went up from the watching crowd, and Dan clapped Mike on the back. Mike grinned at her from across the pool table, then sauntered around to her side to collect his due. He looked down at her, a self-satisfied smirk on his lips. "I believe you owe me something," he said.

She grimaced.

"You're not going to try to get out of it, are you?"

"I always pay my debts," she said in low voice.

The audience hooted and a smattering of clapping followed. Delaney rose up onto tiptoes, put her hands on Mike's shoulders, and pressed a chaste peck to his mouth. The warm feel of his lips stunned her, and the thought sprinted through her mind that she should just kiss him, really kiss him the way she wanted to, audience be damned.

Right, and make an even bigger fool of herself now than she did as a teenager.

She began to pull away, but Mike's hands closed around her waist and pulled her up against him. His body was lean and hard, and the intimacy of the contact made her breath come faster.

"*That* was not a kiss," he said.

The fan club tittered.

"Yes, it was," she protested.

"No it wasn't." He dipped his head toward hers. "*This* is a forfeit kiss," he said. "Pay attention."

8

———

Delaney stiffened, terrified she was about to make a spectacle of herself in front of all these people. But as Mike covered her mouth with his, every coherent thought in her head evaporated.

His lips slid over hers, gently at first, then insistently pushing her to respond. With the smallest of sighs, she let herself relax, let her hands slide up the muscles of his arms and over his shoulders. He pressed her tightly to him and his tongue teased her lips, played with her mouth until she opened to him. And then he kissed her soundly, dragging her with him into a dark, dizzying place. And at the very moment she would have agreed to anything he might have proposed, he let go of her and grinned.

"*That*, Pumpy, was a forfeit kiss," he said, and picked up his beer.

She took a step back and tried to pull herself together, tried to drag her rum-sodden brain back to coherency so she could snap out a clever comeback. But her usually well-ordered thoughts were jumbled beyond rescue.

"Forfeit kiss?" Lauren said loudly. "I think she just paid in advance for her next ten losses!"

The throng roared, then dissipated, everyone going back to what they'd been doing before—drinking, chatting, darts, and more drinking. Cheeks burning, Delaney turned stiffly toward Lauren, her mind trying to make sense of both the intensity of Mike's kiss and her response to it.

"Well, that was quite something," Lauren said with a giggle.

Quite something indeed, Delaney thought. She'd been a spectacle once again. How could she still react to Mike after fifteen years? Other people got over their childhood crushes. Why couldn't she?

She looked for Mike and found him already locked in conversation with Sully, as though a very public passionate kiss was just business as usual for him and, *Step up ladies, who's next?*

As though reading her thoughts, Lauren nodded toward Mike. "You know, he hasn't had a serious relationship since his divorce eight years ago."

"None?"

"Well, he's dated a couple of women. But nothing serious."

No wonder everyone in the bar had been so into the bet. Ah, what did it matter anyway? This was Mike's town, his friends—not hers. Tonight, that had become as crystal clear as champagne glasses etched with the bride and groom's names. She made a show of checking her watch. "I'm going to take off. Too much to do tomorrow."

"I'm right behind you. I can't stay up this late anymore." Lauren stifled a yawn and went to find Dan.

Delaney glanced one more time in Mike's direction, then headed out the door. She couldn't be like this. Couldn't let herself keep thinking wishfully about Mike.

Outside, the clear night sky still glittered with stars, and Delaney looked up to search for Orion's belt, then his arms and legs and the bow he carried. The belt was always easy to find, but spotting the rest took more effort.

God, but the sky was gorgeous tonight. An astronomer's sky. *A lovers' sky.*

She lowered her gaze and cut through the parking lot, forcing herself to bypass her car. No reason to drive, not with her head full of rum and home only a few blocks away.

All she'd wanted when she came to Birch Harbor was to finish the weddings and get her inheritance. That was all. And then Mike had to step in and complicate everything with a kiss that almost felt like it meant something.

Oh, for God's sake, she had to pull it together. That kiss meant nothing at all. She knew that. The guy still called her Pumpy. That alone should be enough to show her how he really felt about her.

Mike paused in his conversation with Sully and looked around for Pumpkin. He hadn't been talking that long; what happened to her?

Lauren touched him on the arm and mouthed, "She left."

He glanced at the door, shocked at his level of disappointment. That made twice in fifteen minutes that he'd been surprised by his response to something Pumpkin had done.

Her kiss had been the first time. The feel of her lips on his, that first little kiss, had made him want to push past her walls. So he'd deepened the kiss. And what he'd gotten was a response so uninhibited he'd taken it to another level ... "She's probably still in the parking lot." Sully rubbed a hand over his abundant chins and raised his thick gray eyebrows.

Dan leaned into the conversation. "Keep up the good work. I knew you had it in you."

"What are you waiting for?" Sully asked.

Both men were encouraging him, but for different reasons. Dan was talking about the Pumpkin project—and Sully was just talking about good old-fashioned attraction. Mike gave a shrug and went outside. He crunched across the gravel parking lot, searching for Pumpkin but finding only her car.

Hell. She must have decided to walk home. He hoped she hadn't gone away mad; it would only make it harder for them to work together. Tomorrow he'd make up some excuse to stop by the shop so he could try to gauge her frame of mind.

***

Early the next morning, Delaney pulled open the door to the waiting room of Hobart & Hobart's. Sounded like a law firm. She stepped across the grimy floor, past the row of molded-plastic chairs along the windows and the table in the corner stacked with faded magazines and a dingy coffeemaker. Not much had changed since Dan's dad had owned the place. Probably the same coffeemaker. Probably even the same magazines. Fortunately, no one would ever mistake this place for a law firm.

She'd just come from Mike's law office, hoping to deliver the sheet music for Sunday's wedding to his assistant, and escape without seeing Mike. But the office had been locked, and a sign on the door said they were out until one and Mike could be found at Hobart & Hobart if something needed immediate attention.

Great. Her plan to avoid him wasn't working out so well. Maybe she'd be lucky and he'd have gone out to pick up coffee or something. She cheered at the thought. If that was the case, she could just leave the music with Dan.

She reached for the door between the waiting room and the garage, then stopped. Maybe she could just call the pianist and have her contact Mike directly about the music.

Yeah, and maybe she should stop being such a chicken and get on with it.

She yanked open the door and spotted Dan in the first bay, bending over the open front end of a long silver car. A black SUV was in the second bay, a white minivan in the third, and she could see the red Chevy in the fourth with its hood open. She let out a slow breath; looked like nobody else was around.

"Hi Dan," she said.

He lifted his head and straightened, an air gun in his hand. "Well, if it isn't our resident pool shark. Remind me not to challenge you at poker. What can I do for you?"

She held up the yellow envelope of sheet music. 'I've got the music for Mike—for the wedding Saturday. A sign on his door said he was here. Can I leave it with you?"

He jerked his thumb over his shoulder. "You can give it to him yourself. He's right over there."

She squinted across the garage. "Where?"

"Where do you think? Under Uncle Henry's car."

Her heartrate sped up.

"You want me to yell for him?"

"No." Delaney reluctantly headed across the garage, past the silver car and the black SUV and the white minivan. She stopped at the Chevy to bend over the open front end and stare at the engine. Then she moved to the side of the car where she could see Mike's feet sticking out from underneath.

"Hey, Mike," she said loud enough to be heard over the sound of Dan's air gun. "I've got that sheet music for the wedding. I'll just leave it on the front—"

Mike shot out from under the car, rolled off the creeper and onto his feet. He grinned, and a thought slipped into her mind unbidden--that his grin came with a kiss and a profession of love ...

Omigod, please stop.

He tugged a faded red rag from the back pocket of his blue work pants and wiped off his hands. She thrust the envelope at him. "If you want to run though the music with the pianist, her number's on the envelope," she said in a rush. "Any time after three today or tomorrow morning works for her. If you don't have time, the wedding rehearsal is six-thirty tomorrow night—I wrote the location on the envelope—and it'll just have to do. I called the bride and she is, believe it or not, okay with you singing. Of course, she does think you do this all the time, so she has a bit of a false sense of security but—"

"And good morning to you, too," he said.

"Oh, sorry. Morning."

He opened the envelope and flipped through the sheets. "If it makes you feel any better, you were right—I know all these songs. A little practice and I'll be ready to go."

"And you actually can sing?" The question sounded harsh spoken out loud and she instantly regretted it.

Thankfully, he laughed. "You want to hear me?"

She clasped her hands together and raised her arms in a circle over her head. "No. I'm happy in my bubble, believing that I've solved this problem. No bubble bursting allowed two days before the wedding."

She slid a hand along the Chevy's gleaming white tail fin. "This is one beautiful car. No wonder you and Dan always wanted it."

"1957 Bel Air convertible. Only forty-seven thousand of these babies were ever made." He took a couple of steps toward the front end. "Has a legendary small-block V-8 engine, generally considered the most famous Chevrolet engine of all time."

She raised her brows. "I'm impressed."

He began to saunter around the car, motioning with his hand and speaking as though he were one of the models on a rotating platform at an auto show. "Power steering. Power brakes. At an overall length of two hundred inches, this car is roomy, fuel-efficient, and tastefully designed with chrome headliner bands on the hardtop, chrome spears on the front fenders, chrome window moldings and—" He pointed at a wheel. "—full chrome wheel covers. Plus—" He paused and leaned into the car to press the horn; the sound echoed against the tall ceilings of the garage. "—a working horn. List price—\$2,238. Can I set you up with one?"

"I'll take two." Delaney laughed.

He studied her for a moment. "You took off quick last night."

A flush crept up her face and she willed it to stop. "It was kind of late. I got to thinking about everything I needed to do today, and decided I'd better get some sleep."

"You weren't upset?"

"About what? It was all harmless fun." No way was she going to let him know the affect his kiss had on her.

"It *was* fun. We should do it again."

She blinked. What? Go to the bar? Play pool? Kiss in front of a large group of spectators?

An awkward silence settled over them. Mike wiped his hands on the rag again. "So, to use some 1950's speak, you want to cruise the avenue? When I get the car drivable?"

Thank God for new topics. "As long as you put the top down. I'll dig out my poodle skirt and bobby socks."

"Okay, we'll go out for a milk shake. Maybe I'll even put the moves on you."

Was Mike Connery flirting with her? Or was he just trying to make up for his actions last night? Did she even want to know?

Yeah, she wanted to know. She wanted to know more than she'd ever wanted to know anything in her life. She looked him square in the eye. "You're on."

9

———

"Thank you for everything!" The bride threw her arms around Delaney. "It was perfect. Everything was perfect! Even the soloist. You were right—he was fantastic."

Delaney hugged her back and restrained the urge to roll her eyes.

"I'm sorry I've been such a pain," the young woman said. "I was just so nervous!"

"You weren't a pain at all," Delaney chirped. What could be more perfect than a cheery white lie on a wedding day?

The bride gave her strapless dress an upward tug, then pranced away to talk to some wedding guests. "Just don't forget to rate me generously on the evaluation form," Delaney muttered.

A yawn escaped her. Amazing that a few days ago she thought she'd never survive this huge wedding, and now it was almost over. It felt like half the town had attended. Dinner for three hundred had been served, the cake—with its exquisite cascade of seashells—had been cut, the garter and bouquet tossed, hours of dancing had taken place, and now the celebration was winding down as the DJ played his last set.

Delaney cast her gaze over the reception hall. All she had left to do was pack up the gifts and her job would be finished. She'd have pulled off the first wedding—well, pulled it off with one hitch, the soloist problem. But as it turned out, that hadn't been a problem at all once Mike took over.

She couldn't believe what a nice voice he had. Hidden all those years in high school behind the mouthpiece of a trumpet. Stifling another yawn, Delaney headed down the hall for the janitor's closet to get some boxes to pack the gifts in. It was hard to believe her ultra-organized great-aunt hadn't put *boxes* on her basic wedding-day checklist. Luckily the facility manager had told her where she could find some.

She opened the door to the closet and tugged the pull-string for the light. A single bare bulb at the ceiling illuminated the room with its harsh glow. Though the overriding smell was one of soap and bleach, the room looked like it hadn't been cleaned in decades. It was also, Delaney noticed, not the treasure trove of boxes the manager had implied. She pushed the door almost shut so she could see the far wall. A single carton lay discarded in the corner, and she went over to retrieve it, tapping it upside down on the floor to dislodge any dust or, worse, spiders.

She began to rummage across the metal shelf units in search of plastic trash bags, and made a mental note to add extra-large garbage bags to her list of necessities. No doubt the list would grow with every wedding she completed.

Spotting the bags behind a big box of cleaner, she threw three into the empty carton, shut off the light, and reached for the door.

"A few more weeks and she's going out of business." A woman's voice floated in from the hallway.

Delaney froze and stared at the barely open door. Were they talking about Storybook Weddings?

Another woman murmured something almost unintelligible. Delaney held her breath and strained to hear, making out the words, "... plenty of time ..." The voice drifted off as the women moved away from the area.

Delany inched closer to the door, staring at the thin shaft of light from the hall cutting across the dark floor of the janitor's closet. Unable to hold her breath any longer, she finally exhaled and gulped in some air. Had that been a couple of locals gossiping? Or was it someone hoping she would fail?

She snorted out a laugh. Or maybe she was overtired and had seen way too many movies.

In the context of a complete conversation, the snippets she'd heard probably meant nothing. Although ... if she could get a glimpse of who had been out there, it might be good information to have. Just in case.

She tucked the box under her arm, dropped her chin, pulled open the door, and charged into the hall. And instantly crashed into someone.

She stumbled back. The box went flying and "Ahahhar!" came out of her mouth as she raised her head. *Mike?*

He grabbed hold of her arms to keep her from falling. "What are you doing?"

So much for surreptitious. "Shush." She put a finger to her lips and jerked Mike into the janitor's closet, shoving the door shut behind them.

"Well, now, this is interesting," he whispered into the darkness. "Don't you think we'd be more comfortable at my place?"

"Don't be ridiculous," she said, as much to herself as to him.

She groped about in the air until her fingers closed around the light string, then gave it a tug. Garish light flooded the room, temporarily blinding them both.

"I didn't hurt your sore wrist, did I?" Mike asked.

"No, it's almost healed. What are you doing here? I thought you went home."

"I think the more logical question is, what are *you* doing here?"

"Listening."

"To what? Mice?"

"To those two women down the hall. I hope they didn't notice it was me coming out of this room."

"The hall was empty," Mike said. "And even if it wasn't, all anyone would've seen was a blur. You got us both into this room so fast, no one could possibly have noticed you leaving. I think I'll start calling you *Flash*." He shook his head. "So what were you listening to?"

She recounted the conversation. "Do you think it means anything?"

"No. Just some busybodies gossiping about how the soloist got sick and I had to take over." He grinned like an excited child. "Did they say anything about how great I sounded?"

She snorted. "No. And the more I think about it, the more I don't think they were gossiping. Their tone was different. More like ..."

"Like ... major league baseball wanting me to sing at the World Series?"

She slapped his arm.

"Like ... music moguls wanting to give me a recording contract?"

"Stop it. This is serious."

"I *am* serious."

"This was more sinister." She nodded to emphasize her words. "They said *she*—so they couldn't have been talking about you. Maybe it has something to do with me. Maybe —" She bit her lip. "Maybe it has to do with the inheritance. About what happens if I don't complete the weddings, if any one of us fails in our tasks."

"Then all the money goes to Ellie's brother, Joe. And I'd like to point out he doesn't need the money so he has no motive. Not to mention the people you overheard were female, right?"

"Yeah."

"As far as conspiracy theories go, this one feels pretty weak. The soloist got sick, that's all. Don't go looking for enemies on every corner." Mike pulled open the door. "Come on, let's get out of here."

Delaney followed him into the hall and stopped to pick up the box she'd dropped. "So what *are* you doing here? It's almost midnight. I thought you went home after dinner."

"Hell, with all your spy antics, you almost made me forget. I came back to show you something." He withdrew a folded sheet of paper from the inside chest pocket of his jacket and handed it to her.

Delaney set the box on the floor and unfolded the sheet. "The bride's evaluation form? She turned it in already? I didn't think we'd see it for at least a week."

"Apparently they were so pleased with the wedding, the mother filled the form out during the reception, then called the executor. He's out of town, so he called me. He thought we might want to get it right away—"

"Before they had a chance to reevaluate their ratings in the cold light of morning. He was right about that." Delaney skimmed to the bottom where the final score was marked. She'd passed with flying colors!

A delighted laugh slipped out of her. She threw her arms around Mike, then danced away. "I feel like I just passed my first-quarter exams."

"Congratulations. And you have a whole week before the next one."

"You know, I have to admit, this wasn't as bad as I thought it would be. Thanks for all your help." She reached to shake his hand. "Especially for singing on such short notice."

"What's this? Do I hear a touch of enthusiasm for wedding planning from Pumpkin McBride?"

"Ahh, let's not get carried away. What you see is a touch of enthusiasm because I'm one step closer to getting my inheritance." *And one step closer to getting my finances in control and my life back where I want it.*

———

Early Monday morning, Mike swung into the Hobart & Hobart to find Dan and Joe Waverly bent over the engine of the old Chevy. Joe's pug was bouncing at their feet, wrapping its leash around their ankles. Mike stepped toward them, his leather-soled loafers making hardly a noise on the floor. "Hey, what's up?" he asked.

"Just showing Joe the resident classic." Dan extricated himself from the leash around his legs.

"Used to have a Bel Air Coupe myself," Joe said. "This sure brings back memories. Mine was all black—black and chrome. What a car. I wasn't smart enough to hang on to it, though. Be worth a pretty penny today if I had."

Mike nodded, a touch of suspicion clouding his thoughts. *Yeah, just like this one would be when it was done.* "These old cars are hard to find now."

The dog tried to jump up on him and Mike shook him off. Stupid mutt.

Joe moved slowly around the car with Dan at his side. "Looks like you're making real progress on the restoration."

"Slow but sure," Mike said. "We're getting there."

"Brake liners today. And new tires," Dan said. "We're almost ready for a test drive."

"It's going to be a beauty. If you two ever want to sell it, let me know."

Mike exchanged a glance with Dan. "Not a chance. We've wanted this car for too long," he said.

"You boys are lucky. I should have hung on to mine," Joe repeated, running a hand over the trunk. "I hear Stonewall and Sully aren't doing so well with their project. The usual personality clashes."

"At least they're speaking," Mike said.

Dan coughed. "Shouting, anyway. It's a start."

Joe raised an eyebrow. "You want me to talk to them? I've known those guys a long time."

So much for suspicions ... and Pumpkin's conspiracy theory. Joe wouldn't offer to step in if he wanted them to fail. "Sure, we'll take any help we can get. Thanks."

"Don't mention it. I'll give them both a call once I get to the office." He headed through the open overhead garage door, the pug prancing beside him on its leash.

"I'll let you know when your Lexus is ready," Dan called after him.

Mike waited until Joe was well up the street before asking, "How'd you end up showing him the car?"

"He came in for an oil change and wanted to see it."

"He did?"

Dan lifted a set of keys off the rack on the wall and squinted at Mike as if he'd lost his mind. "Everyone asks about that car."

"Right. He want to know anything else?"

"No. Like what?"

"I don't know. Pumpkin overheard some women talking and thinks there might be a ..." It dawned on him that he was about to sound as ridiculous as Pumpkin had in the janitor's closet.

"A what?"

Mike winced. "A plot ... to keep us from meeting the terms of the will."

"A plot. Of course. And the Russians are behind it?"

"Maybe Joe Waverly."

Dan choked on a laugh. "Never in a million years. He doesn't need the money and he'd never do it."

"That's what I said. So, humor me here. He didn't say anything suspicious?'

Dan feigned shock. "Now that I've had a second to think about it ... right after he said he needed an oil change, he said something like, *Hey, Dan, I'm trying to deep-six everyone's inheritance, but you have to promise not to tell anyone. Pinky swear—*"

"Okay. I get it."

"Then he laid out the entire plan for me."

"I get it."

"You don't seriously think he's working that angle, do you?' Dan popped open the hood on a Toyota Camry and checked the oil.

"No."

"Because if you did, I'd have to seriously question your sanity."

10

A CAR HORN BLARED IN FRONT OF THE WEDDING SHOP and Delaney glanced up from her to-do list. Didn't people know they weren't supposed to blow their horns unless it was an emergency? She bent over her list again, only to be startled by the sound once more. This time the horn beat out a rhythm. She pushed her chair back and went to the wide storefront window.

Out in front, Mike was leaning against the driver's door of Uncle Henry's red Chevy. The convertible top was down, the sleeves of his white T-shirt were rolled up, and an unlit cigarette dangled from his mouth. Shades of James Dean in *Rebel without a Cause.*

He flexed a bicep. She laughed and stepped outside into the bright sunlight.

"Hey, baby." He pulled the cigarette out of his mouth. "Dream as if you'll live forever. Live as if you'll die today," he said, grinning.

He knew James Dean.

Married. A child. Divorced. A James Dean fan, *like her*. How much more did she not know about this man?

'You want to go for a spin?"

"I thought you'd never ask. Just let me lock up." She ran into the shop to grab her keys.

Back outside, Mike popped open the passenger door for her, then sauntered around to slide into the driver's seat and rev the engine a couple of times.

"Impressed?" he asked.

"Not exactly." She laughed at his stricken expression.

"I did all this and I'm not making any points?" He put the car into gear and pulled away from the curb.

The breeze tousled her hair. "You're making points, don't worry. Although I'm not so sure about the cigarette ..."

He pulled it from his mouth and held it out to her. Just a cylinder of rolled paper, held tight with a piece of scotch tape.

"Nice." She handed it back and hooked a thumb over her shoulder at the empty space where the backseat should have been. "I see the restoration isn't quite finished."

"Not hardly. But once we fixed the brakes and put on new tires, I couldn't resist taking her out for a ride. Especially when it's a warm spring day and there's a beautiful woman down the street I want to impress."

She tried to think of something witty to say, but discovered all of her brain cells were too caught up in his flattery to formulate a reply. So she settled for just grinning inanely.

Mike pulled the car into the ice-cream parlor at the edge of town. Once they each had a chocolate shake in hand, they set off down the highway.

"So where are we going?" Delaney sucked a mouthful of shake through the fat red straw.

"You'll see."

"Hmm. A mystery. Have I been there before?"

He pursed his lips. "Based on your age when you moved out of town, I would guess the answer is ... maybe."

"And it's okay if we have milk shakes with us?"

"No problem at all."

She dropped her head back and raised her face to the glorious blue sky. The wind whipped across her cheeks and tossed her hair and she realized she hadn't experienced this feeling of freedom in a long time.

"Makes you feel like a kid, doesn't it?" he said.

Yeah. Like she was seventeen and Mike had finally, *finally* noticed she was alive. Too bad fifteen years and a lot of water had gone under the bridge since then. Because all her naiveté about the permanence of relationships had long since washed away.

Mike reached across to put an arm around her shoulders and pull her close. "We may as well do this right," he said.

Delaney took another draw of her milk shake. Even all that water under the bridge couldn't dampen the thrill she was getting from riding in a classic convertible, with the top down and Mike's arm around her.

After several minutes they turned onto a narrow paved road leading into a state forest—the road to Sunset Point, the place where every teenager in the know went to park. "Figure out where we're going yet?"

"It's a little early, isn't it?" She laughed and brushed the hair off her face.

"So you *have* been out here."

"No, I was far too chaste when I lived in Birch Harbor. And you? How much time did you spend at the point?"

"Well ..." He took a drink of his shake.

"Are you hedging?" she teased.

"No. Counting."

"Counting? As in number of girls?" She jabbed his shoulder and he let out a laugh. "Humph. Take me home." She sat back against the passenger door and crossed her arms over her chest, feigning offense.

"Too late," he said.

They pulled out of the woods into a parking lot along a high scenic overlook; the waters of Green Bay shimmered below them in the afternoon sun. Mike shut off the engine and pushed open his door. "Welcome to Sunset Point. Come on."

He grabbed her hand and pulled her into the woods, not appearing to follow any discernible path. "Hey, Meriwether Lewis, where are we going?" she asked.

"Just follow me." He picked his way through the underbrush, stepping over muddy patches and ducking below low-hanging branches. The smell of moist wood and dirt, of the spring forest in the shade, filled her senses.

Milk shake in hand, she followed Mike without speaking. After ten minutes of steady downhill hiking, they broke out of the woods onto a dirt-and-rock outcropping. She gasped. Green Bay stretched out in front of them as expansive as a sea, the sun glittering on the deep blue surface like gems on a velvet display cloth. Far below, waves lapped gently on a narrow sand beach.

"This is incredible. How did you find it?"

Mike reached over to pull some leaves from her hair. As

his fingers brushed against her cheek, their eyes met. "Dan and I discovered it in high school."

She rolled her eyes. "Let me guess. Bringing girls down here?"

He gave her a sheepish grin. "We were trying to find a path to the beach. Figured it would really impress our dates —you know, a private spot, a blanket on the sand, a bottle of cheap wine. Way more romantic than making out in the car."

He was right about that. "Did you find a path all the way down?"

"Gets too steep. The lake has undercut a lot of the cliff." He sat on the rock shelf, legs stretched out in front, then leaned back on his hands.

"Once you found this place, it probably didn't matter that you couldn't get to the beach," Delaney said with a smile. She tried to spot the scenic overlook above them, but could see nothing but rocks and trees.

He followed her gaze. "You can't see down here from up there. It's totally private."

"How *convenient* for high-school boys." She sat cross-legged beside him, one bare knee accidentally brushing his thigh. "This hard ground, though ... not real conducive to making out."

"We planned ahead." Mike grinned and put a hand on her knee.

Her breath caught. "Oh, don't tell me." She forced a light laugh.

"Yeah. We kept a couple of blankets down here sealed in plastic garbage bags."

"Oh my God, I can't believe it. Well, actually, yes I can."

"Come on, we were guys. Seventeen and eighteen years old."

"Nineteen, twenty ..."

"Okay, guilty as charged. But I haven't brought anyone here in years. Except Andie. And she just thinks it's a fun place for a picnic that Dan and I found while exploring as kids."

And me, Delaney's mind whispered, *you just brought me out here.*

He looked at her as though he'd just had the same thought. And then the moment stretched too long and she made herself glance away.

"Do you ever regret moving back? Leaving Chicago?" Her hand trembled slightly as she sipped her shake, now more like thick chocolate milk than ice cream.

He shook his head. "It's the best place for Andie to grow up. And I like being in charge of my time. In Chicago, other people owned me. I worked for a high-profile firm doing mergers and acquisitions."

"And you don't miss the excitement of it?" She couldn't imagine never again experiencing the exhilaration she got from advertising. She shifted her leg farther away from his.

"You mean the long hours and the stress? No. When Andie's mom took a job out of the country, it seemed like the right time to make a change, simplify. My daughter was eight years old. I wanted to be able to go to her spring recitals, be there when she *flew up* from Brownies to Girl Scouts."

Delaney tried not to gape. "You're sounding too good to be true."

"Well, okay, I didn't really *want* to attend the fly-up ceremony. But she wanted me there, so ..." He lifted one shoulder in a shrug.

He still sounded too good to be true.

Luckily, unlike her mother, Delaney had learned early in life that if something seemed too good to be true, it usually was. Especially where men were concerned. Her mother had spent a lifetime searching for her white knight, never realizing that inside every suit of shining armor was just another mortal man who would let her down.

She'd vowed never to repeat her mother's mistake. No matter what the guy looked like, no matter how charming his words, no matter how much the sight of him made her heart pound.

"I can't even imagine permanently leaving the advertising world," she said. "After being off work for three months, I'm chomping at the bit to get back in."

Mike gave her a sideways glance. "Three months? Did I miss something? You've only been here a week."

She dropped her chin. "I probably should have told you right away, but it's not the kind of thing you want to announce, you know?" She drew a breath and exhaled. "I got laid off when the agency where I worked lost the client that I was the account executive for."

He couldn't believe it. Delaney needed this inheritance as much as the rest of them did—maybe even more. She wasn't on a leave of absence; he didn't have to romance her to get her to stay long enough to finish the weddings. He'd taken her for a drive today, brought her to Sunset Point as part of the plan. He'd even figured he'd kiss her again today. But now, he didn't have to.

He looked at her mouth, at her softly parted lips, and remembered Wednesday night in the bar. He jerked his thoughts back to the present. "I didn't realize you were out of work. I know some advertising guys in Green Bay I could call if you're interested."

Her eyebrows arched. "Uh, thanks. But, no, I don't think so."

"Not worldly enough, huh?"

"Oh, no. Well ... yeah. Bigger cities mean bigger clients." She laughed self-consciously.

He'd suspected as much the first day he talked to her on the phone. Delaney McBride had big fish to fry in places far from here. She was way beyond Birch Harbor.

He thought about what it had been like to kiss her, how she'd felt pressed against him, his hands in her silky hair. No. None of that mattered. He'd come home to simplify his life. And getting involved with Delaney would only add complication. Because to her, the life he'd chosen didn't look simplified. It merely looked simple.

"Ready to go back to work?" he asked.

She nodded and scrambled to her feet, leading the way to the path into the woods. As he watched her go, realization hit him like a line drive to the head—he wanted to kiss her again.

11

THE HEIRS' MEETING WAS GOING NOWHERE FAST. Delaney set her elbows on the library's conference table and bit her tongue for the third time in half an hour as Mike tried to get the Henrys back on track. And they ignored him again. The two men seemed to take an almost perverse delight in antagonizing each other. She was beginning to wonder whether the group would be better off meeting somewhere public. At least the Henrys might be embarrassed into behaving themselves.

"Stonewall, you haven't got the brains God gave wild geese." Sully gestured at the other Henry with a fat fingered hand as though pronouncing a royal edict.

Stonewall drew his bushy brows together and crossed his arms over his chest. "When God was passing out the brains," he said in a condescending drawl, "you thought he said *trains* and hopped a ride out of town."

"Guys," Mike said, "we need a report. What's your progress on the band shell? Are you on target to meet the deadline?"

Both men started talking at once. Mike held up a hand. "One at a time. Stonewall, you first."

"The thing is, we need to do this right. And there's not enough time for that. How are we supposed to—"

"That attitude is what's the problem," Sully interrupted. "Every time we try to settle something, Stonewall, well, stonewalls it. What about this? What about that? He sees more roadblocks than—"

"Listen, guys—" Mike shoved back his chair and stood. "You have got to find a way to work together."

"I only ask questions to make sure we do this right," Stonewall shot out.

"Do it right? You mean as in, *do it your way*." Sully shook his head.

Lauren cleared her throat. "You know, there's often not just one right way or a wrong way—"

"And just what's wrong with my way?"

"Okay, time-out," Mike made the referee hand signal.

Delaney appreciated the diplomacy Mike was using to get these guys to work together. She especially appreciated how hard it must be for him not to launch an F-bomb at them. But she had a wedding in just two days for which she'd already put out a fire this afternoon, and she had no time for ridiculous arguments.

"What is wrong with you Henrys?" she demanded. Every head in the room spun toward her. "This is only our second meeting and the two of you have fought through both of them like spoiled children." Her phone vibrated in her back pocket, but she ignored it. "I don't know what's behind all this animosity and, frankly, I don't care. We all have jobs to do. I'm doing mine. Mike and Dan are doing theirs. Do you expect me to believe that Aunt Eleanor and Uncle Henry would have appreciated you acting this way?"

She crossed her arms over her chest just as Stonewall had, feeling like a substitute teacher in front of an out-of-control class. Her phone vibrated again. "What I'd really like to know is whether you're going to do the job or not. Because I'm not exactly loving this wedding planning thing, and if you're not going to do your part, then I've had enough right now. Do I make myself clear?"

She could see shocked expressions all around, Mike's included. Good. She pulled out her phone to check the missed call and spotted the number for one of her former coworkers. Probably just checking in; Delaney had called her on the drive to Birch Harbor. Still ...

"I've got to return this call," she said, standing. "While I'm gone, Stonewall and Sully, you figure out what you're doing. If you're planning to quit, you need to decide that now, not next month. Because if that's the case, my career as a wedding planner is over as well. I'll expect an answer when I return."

She stalked out of the meeting room to the sound of dead silence, strode past the checkout desk and through the main door. As the last rays of the young summer sun cast their pale light on the library steps, she punched in the code to her voice mail. The scent of a nearby lilac bush in full bloom sent her right back to childhood, to running through town barefoot, hot on Mike's heels and deliriously happy. Her anger at the Henrys gentled. The two men were well into retirement; they probably didn't thrive under tight deadlines and pressure like she did.

Caroline's voicemail pulled her from her reverie. "*Hey,*

Delaney, how's wedding planning? You're not going to believe this—Jack had lunch with the marketing director at Avalon Cosmetics and they're already not happy with the new agency. Doesn't mean they're coming back or anything, but at least you're sort of vindicated. Other than that ... same old, same old. Long hours, big presentations, low pay. Call me when you can break away from the brides!"

Delaney leaned against the brick wall of the library and replayed the message. Back at the agency, the place she belonged, they were making things happen. They were kicking butt and taking names. If she were there, she'd be taking part in brainstorming meetings, creating advertising campaigns, working long hours to pull together client proposals. But instead, she was stuck in Weddingville, where, yes, she would be putting in long hours—arranging for a flock of white doves to be released at exactly the moment the church bells chimed at exactly the moment the bride said *I do.*

She went into the *recent calls* screen and swiped across Caroline's number. "They're not happy?" she asked the moment her friend answered. "Did I predict this or what?"

Caroline let out a laugh. "You didn't hear this from me, but supposedly Jack is working it."

Delaney sat on the library steps. "God, would I love to be in on this."

"Who knows? If it goes anywhere, maybe you will be."

Delaney's smile came slowly. She would give just about anything to be back there and part of the action again. "Too bad I've got all these weddings to plan. And brides and their mothers to keep happy." *Yeehaw.*

"Well, nothing's happening yet. They only had lunch

today. And, who knows, the guy could be stroking Jack to make him feel better about losing the account."

"Yeah. Well, keep me posted."

"I'll put in a word for you if it looks like it's coming to anything. So, tell me, how are you liking wedding planning?"

After chatting a few more minutes, they ended the call. Delaney knew she should go back into the heirs meeting, but she couldn't get herself to move while she was still processing everything Caroline had told her. Realistically, it wasn't likely that Avalon would dump their new agency and return to the old. It would waste too much time and money, cause too much second-guessing. And even if they did, there was no guarantee Delaney would be asked to return as account executive.

She fixed her gaze on the sky overhead, streaked with deep blues and pink and gold. Annoyance skittered through her. She didn't want lovely sunsets; she wanted back into advertising.

The library door opened and she turned to see Mike stalking toward her, his mouth pressed into a tight line. He paused at the top of the steps. "Way to go, Dale Carnegie. How to win friends and influence people."

She huffed. She didn't want to hear a lecture about dealing with the Henrys.

"It just took me ten minutes to undo the damage you caused so the Henrys will keep working together. You have no idea how hard it was to get them to agree to do this in the first place." He dropped down beside her.

She forced herself not to move away from him. Her world was crappy enough right now. The last thing she needed was Mike telling her how bad she was and making it worse. "They cause their own damage."

"Those two guys lost one of their best friends."

"Years ago."

"No matter. They were a threesome."

"I know all about it. The 3-H Club—cello, violin and piano."

"No, they were more than that—golf, poker, fishing, you name it. Then Henry Clark died. And that left these two, who never got along very well in the first place."

"So now they hate each other? It doesn't make sense."

"Everybody grieves in their own way and time, Pumpkin." He patted her knee and she clenched her jaw at the patronizing gesture.

"All I know is, it's Thursday night," she said evenly. "I have a rehearsal dinner to oversee tomorrow night. And an even bigger wedding to pull off this weekend than last."

"And all *I* know is if we want to get our inheritances, we can't go around pissing each other off. So let me give you a piece of wisdom learned from my years in law. You can catch more flies with honey than with vinegar."

An acid-laced retort leaped to the tip of her tongue, but before she could let loose with it, he was already standing.

"Now, Pumpy, let's go finish the meeting because I'm sure everyone's getting restless in there."

Pumpy? *Pumpy?* She'd had enough of being Pumpy. She'd had enough of trying to figure out why he'd never gotten past the fat redhead she used to be. Who did he think he was?

She stood and leveled a cold stare on him. "No, Mikey, I don't think so. I don't need your lectures, I don't need your sympathy, I don't need your rah-rah cheerleading." Suddenly, she realized, she wasn't sure she even liked this adult Mike at all. Maybe she'd never liked who he was, just the image of who she wanted him to be. How could she ever have thought herself attracted to him? "And I really don't need to be Pumpy McBride anymore. Have you ever given any thought to what it felt like—feels like—to be called Pumpkin when you're red-haired and fat?"

He stared at her.

"No. I didn't think so." Oh, this felt good. "Frankly, I've had quite enough of tonight's heirs' meeting if you don't mind." She took off down the sidewalk purposefully, covering long stretches of concrete with her strides, knowing that Mike was watching her go. *Let him watch my back. Let him watch me walk right out of this town and out of his life.* She tossed her hair dramatically.

Not that she was in his life anyway. And not that she could leave this town before the weddings were done and her inheritance secured. Her steps faltered and slowed. She felt as if she were in a movie and any minute the hero should chase her down the sidewalk and stop her, tell her how sorry he was and beg her to stay.

But at the end of the second block, she resigned herself to the fact that life just wasn't that well scripted. And this town sure as hell was no movie set.

Head down, hands in her jacket pockets, she hurried toward the wedding shop. Much as she wanted to chuck wedding planning for the night, she knew she'd better check the shop's messages. She'd been out most of the afternoon with last-minute appointments: watching the bride hang on for dear life while practicing sidesaddle horseback riding at

Lucky C Stables in preparation for Saturday's ceremony; meeting with the restaurant manager to confirm the seating and menu for the rehearsal dinner; clearing up confusion at the bakery about a supposed cancellation of the cake order ... Luckily, she'd been able to rectify the cake mistake without much trouble.

Still, with a bride she'd privately taken to calling Bridezilla, this event would be nothing if not a challenge.

She stepped into the office and pointed a finger at the red light blinking on the answering machine. "I forbid you to be anything but good news." Pen in hand, she settled into the desk chair and hit *play*, fully expecting yet another frantic call from the bride-to-be. Sunday morning couldn't come fast enough.

"Hi, Delaney. This is Tina at Floral Fantasies," a woman said. "It's Thursday about five. I hate to leave this on the answering machine, but I've tried to call you a couple of times already."

Her serious tone made Delaney uneasy. She hadn't given anyone her cell phone number because, well, this wasn't her real job and, besides, her aunt's meticulous planning made it seem unnecessary. Hopefully that hadn't been a mistake.

"We've had something of a disaster."

Delaney's stomach began to churn.

"When I came in this morning, I discovered our cooler had malfunctioned and our flowers, everything we had, froze. All our roses, carnations and daisies. All those lovely calla lilies and orchids ruined. I didn't call you because the wholesaler said they could deliver replacements today. But I've just received the order and—" Tina drew an audible breath "—the orchids are the wrong color and the callas aren't there. Since it's last minute and June, I can't even get enough of the blooms your bride wants from the Milwaukee wholesaler. Too many other weddings ..." The woman's voice quivered. "I can get a lot of different flowers right away, just not all the ones she wanted. Maybe the bride would be okay with something else. Please give me a call as soon as you get this. I'll keep trying to reach you."

The machine clicked off and Delaney set the pen on the pad of paper. Tears leaped to her eyes and she squeezed them back. The wedding was at one o'clock, the day after tomorrow. Now she had thirty-six hours to figure out the flowers? How could she call the bride and ask if she'd take something else? She hadn't nicknamed the woman Bridezilla because she was easy to work with.

She hit *play* again, then slumped into her chair and closed her eyes.

12

———

MIKE STOOD IN THE DOORWAY TO THE SHOP'S OFFICE and watched Delaney as the message played. Watched the soft light from the desk lamp highlight the golden strands in her red hair. He'd known from the first moment he'd heard her on the phone that Pumpkin McBride had grown up. But he'd never taken the time to consider the woman she'd become—and what she had gone through to get there. Not when Dan proposed he romance Pumpkin to keep her in town. Not even when he reluctantly agreed to do it. And especially not minutes ago when he'd treated her like a wayward child in need of his expert guidance.

"Hey, Delaney?"

She jerked her head up and punched the *off* button on the answering machine. "How does everyone get in this store without jangling the bell?"

He shrugged apologetically.

"Aren't you supposed to be at the heirs' meeting?" she asked.

"We adjourned early again. Seem to have a real

problem finishing those meetings." He stepped into the room. "I just wanted to say I'm sorry. And if you don't want my lectures or my sympathy or my cheerleading, much as it breaks my heart, I understand." He smiled sheepishly. "And, well, how about if I never call you Pumpkin again?"

She looked at him for what seemed like a full minute, her expression unreadable. "That would be a start."

"And I'll never give you advice again, unless you ask for it."

She just kept looking at him. "And you'll never bring up vinegar and honey."

"Never."

"Or Dale Carnegie," she said.

"Or Dale Carnegie."

"Or any derivative of Pumpkin."

"Or any derivative of Pumpkin," he said quietly.

She nodded and dropped her gaze.

"We never meant any harm. Not then. Not now. Pumpkin was mostly because of the red hair. Just like they called me 007 because my last name was Connery. And Dan was Hobes because his last name was Hobart. And Jack Turleton was Spike—"

"Because of his grandstanding in the football games. Yeah, I know. I get it All the guys had nicknames. All the guys and me, the fat redhead."

"No. Just *the redhead*. So what do you say, Delaney? Will you forgive me if I promise never to screw up again?"

In the subdued light he saw the vulnerability in her expression, and for just a second, the young girl whose heart had always been big enough to forgive the transgressions against her. And then the girl was gone. Delaney rolled her eyes and stuck out a hand. "Don't get carried away. You're a man. You'll screw up again."

"What? Delaney, you cut me to the quick." He clasped her hand and she flashed him a quick grin. And he realized all he wanted to do was pull her into his arms and press his mouth to hers. He waved at the answering machine and dropped into the extra chair beside her desk. "Let's hear that message again."

Delaney played it twice more, as though the repetition might provide an answer. Then she called the florist. As much as he'd been irritated by Delaney's words at the heirs' meeting, Mike couldn't help admiring how she took charge of the conversation, patiently searching for a solution even though it was clear there would be no quick fix.

She shook her head. "I don't know how my aunt handled the stress. In just two weddings I've already had three crises. The singer got laryngitis. Then the cake fiasco. And now this. That's not even taking into consideration what it's like dealing with the brides. God knows what lies ahead."

"What cake fiasco?"

"Oh, you'll enjoy this," Delaney said. "I stopped in the bakery today to confirm they'd be bringing an assortment of petit fours along with the cake. Somehow they thought we'd canceled the cake. Said someone called."

"Why would anyone cancel the wedding cake?"

"Exactly. Obviously they got the orders mixed up. Anyway, everything's fine. We'll have both a cake and petit fours on Saturday."

Mike let his head drop back against the chair. "I'm feeling your wedding planning pain. So, what's the verdict with the flowers? Listening to your end of the call, I got the impression the only option was to fly them in from a tropical island."

"Close. We can get everything we need from a wholesaler in Chicago. But they can't deliver until end of workday tomorrow."

Mike ran a hand through his hair. "Way too late. Doesn't leave time to arrange them."

"Right. Tina would drive down and pick them up, but she's got too many orders to redo for other events."

"How about talking the bride into switching flowers?"

"Bridezilla? Not a chance. If I force this on her, it would pretty much guarantee an unsatisfactory rating."

"Game over." He picked up a pencil from Delaney's desktop and twirled it in his fingers as he contemplated their options.

Delaney nodded. "But, all is not lost yet. The wholesaler opens at seven a.m. It'll take four-and-a-half hours to get there. If I time this right, I can arrive when the doors open."

"Up all night and then drive back on no sleep?"

"Ever hear of caffeine?"

"Ever hear of falling asleep at the wheel?" he said. "Or breaking down? The side of the highway at three in the morning is not a good place for a woman alone."

Delaney paced across the small office. "I told Tina I could help her arrange the flowers. But I have to get them here first."

She wasn't listening to him. "How about using a delivery service?" he suggested.

"Yeah, except to get the flowers here by noon would cost

a fortune. And with my luck, something would go wrong. Sometimes it's just best to do things yourself. I'm sure Tina would let me use the Floral Fantasies van." She stopped and looked at him. "I'm going to Chicago. Tonight."

"I'll go with you."

"No need. You've got legal things to do tomorrow." She gave him a dismissive wave.

"Yeah, but this is more important. We'll be home by noon, anyway."

She began to shake her head, and he held up a hand. "No arguments. Andie's at my folks right now—I'll swing over there and make sure she can stay overnight. You get the van. I'll meet you back here at one."

———

Sometime after four in the morning, Delaney steered the old white van onto the Milwaukee bypass. Lights flashed across the windows as she passed by the few other cars on the highway and the brightly lit signs above stores and restaurants that had closed hours ago. The van felt like a cocoon, a haven against the dark emptiness just outside its doors.

She drank some coffee from her insulated mug and peeked over at Mike, sleeping, curled into a pillow against the door. She was glad he'd insisted on coming along; it was reassuring to not be alone, to have someone else, another driver, with her.

Mike's breathing came even and slow, and she wondered what it would be like to wake up with him in the morning, have him roll over and wrap her in his arms and kiss her to consciousness. He shifted against the window, and she gripped the steering wheel more tightly and concentrated on the road.

The van's headlights glared across a police car hidden under an overpass, nakedly exposing its truth for being there—a radar speed gun pointed out of the driver's window.

All things had a truth—you just had to look deep enough and be open to finding it.

Just as ... Mike's kiss in the bar had been a forfeit kiss and nothing more.

Just as ... the twelve new dresses she'd found in her mother's closet after her death were actually a lesson to be learned. Twelve brand-new elegant pastel dresses, each with the tags still on, each bought by her mother to get remarried in, a new dress every time she thought she'd met the man of her dreams. Twelve dresses that exposed her mother's desperation, revealed a lifetime spent searching for a man to rely on and belong with—and never finding him.

Mike's phone blared the William Tell Overture from deep in the pocket where he'd stashed it. He startled awake and cleared his throat a couple of times before swiping a finger across the screen and croaking out, "Hello?" He rubbed a hand across his eyes. "Cassie, it's the middle of the night."

Cassie?

"I'm driving to Chicago." A pause and then, "Because I need to be there at seven in the morning. Everything's fine. Andie's with my parents. I got your message, just forgot to call you back. It's been a wild night." He sat silent for another minute. "I'm sure she'll be excited. You'll be back for how long?"

Delaney locked her hands on the steering wheel. Was this Andie's mom? Mike's former wife?

"You can tell her yourself. She'll be home after three." By the tone of Mike's voice, he was trying to wrap up the call. "Okay, fine, I'll tell her." He sounded disappointed. "Yeah. Thanks for calling." He swiped off the call and slouched back into the pillow.

"My ex-wife," he said. "In Berlin. It's six hours later there."

"I take it she's worried?"

He shrugged. "I guess. She left a message earlier. She's coming back for the first two weeks of August."

"Andie will be excited, I'm sure."

"Yeah, but God forbid she interrupt whatever she's got going on tomorrow to call Andie and deliver the news herself."

"Maybe she doesn't have a choice." Delaney knew what it was like to have a demanding job.

"I guess. Like I said before, she's pretty high-powered. Important."

Delaney could tell from his voice that he wasn't impressed.

Mike shifted his position against the door. "We were law students when we met—and stupid. She got pregnant. We married. Had a baby. Graduated law school. Passed the bar exam. Got jobs." His voice softened. "Started making a life together."

Envy softly seeped into Delaney. She knew the answer

to her next question even before she asked it. "Did you love her?"

"Yeah. I loved her a lot."

She reached toward him and he grasped her hand. "I'm sorry," she said, really meaning it. "I wish it had worked out for you." Regardless of what she believed about happily ever after, she actually did wish love would work out for someone.

"Cassie used to say if she wanted to get to the top, she had to put in twice the hours as anyone else in the office."

"That's kind of what women are up against." Delaney knew it well.

She changed lanes and passed a lone car on the highway. Now that they were past the city with its overhead lights and neon signs, the night seemed darker, the sky lower.

Mike took an Oreo cookie from the package on the floor, twisted it apart and put half in his mouth. "I came home from work one day to find Andie in her high chair eating Cheerios, and Cassie at the kitchen table drinking a martini with three fat olives on the swizzle stick. We started talking, and every time she made an important point, she sucked down one of those olives."

"You don't have to tell me this."

"It's okay." He jammed the rest of the Oreo into his mouth. "Olive number one—she didn't love me, and we never should have married just because she was pregnant. Olive number two—she was leaving. And olive number three ..." He hesitated a moment. "I could have custody of the baby."

Delaney sucked in a gasp. A lump welled up in her

throat at his and Andie's loss. "Mike ... how can you stand it?"

He shrugged. "I got this great kid out of the deal. We're a pretty good team. The rest? You just file it away. What other choice is there? Some things it's best not to think about."

Delaney watched the broken white center line as though it marked a route she was supposed to follow, a never-ending path that led to God knew where. For Mike, it had rescued him away from the pain of his marriage and brought him back to Birch Harbor. But for her, all it seemed to be was an arrow pointing directly toward Boston.

She took the next off-ramp, pulled into a gas station and filled up the tank. It was Mike's turn to drive. She needed to sleep. Because sleep was the only way she'd be able keep from dwelling on the fact that Mike had never gotten over his ex-wife.

13

Back in Birch Harbor later that morning, Delaney dropped Mike at his car, then sped over to the florist shop. Tina hurried out the front door, her short gray hair looking like she hadn't combed it in two days.

"You made it!" She brought her hands together with a clap. "I tried not to worry about whether there'd be any more problems. Just worked hard all morning, so everything else is caught up." She pulled open the back doors of the van. "They had everything we ordered?"

"Ready and waiting when we got there. We double checked it all before we left."

"And you can still help?" Tina took a box of flowers and led the way to the cooler. "Lauren is coming over to help, too."

"I can't claim any experience or skill, but my hands and mind are willing. I'll work all night if we have to, just as long as these flowers are ready before morning."

"It shouldn't take *all* night." Tina smiled and her face creased into rows of soft folds.

"Wonderful. Because I'm feeling a little sleep-deprived right now." She set a box of flowers on the cooler floor. A shiver rippled through her. "It's downright freezing in here."

"Not quite. Forty degrees. That temperature keeps the flowers fresh." Tina pointed at the thermostat on the wall inside the door. "There's our culprit."

"The cause of all our troubles. Seventy-five degrees outside and forty in here."

She helped Tina bring in the rest of the boxes. "Have you ever had that happen before? The thermostat malfunction?"

Tina stilled. "Never. Not once in all my years of being in business. But, like everything, there's always a first time." She collected an assortment of calla lilies, roses, and orchids and brought them out of the cooler to the butcher block worktable. "What I'm going to do is put together one of the centerpieces so you have a sample to follow. Then you can get started." She took several identical clear vases from a box on the floor.

Delaney's mouth turned down in a frown. "So did they say what caused the problem? It couldn't happen again, could it?"

"It won't happen again because nothing was wrong with it. It didn't malfunction, somehow it got turned down. Now, watch me, here's what you do ..." She quickly demonstrated how to trim the stems at a forty-five-degree angle under running water and arrange them in the vase with ferns and baby's breath. "Just like that, you go from individual flowers to a work of art." She stood back to view her creation.

"That simple, huh?" Delaney asked. She'd been so busy

trying to figure out how the thermostat *somehow* got turned down, she hadn't been paying close attention.

Tina nodded. "We'll need thirty-five of those. I'll get started on the bridesmaids' bouquets."

"Okay." Delaney picked up a purple orchid and eyed it dubiously. Creative insecurity set in. Thirty-five professional-looking centerpieces? She wasn't sure she could do that fully rested, let alone on just a few hours of sleep. God help them all if the bride took notice.

Slipping her fingers into the sheers, she cut the orchid's stem and set it in a vase. She studied the example Tina had put together, then added another orchid, a white calla lily, and some baby's breath. Fabulous. "So I'm just wondering," she asked as she trimmed another orchid, "if nothing was wrong with the thermostat, how did it get turned down?"

Tina let out a slow exhale. "All I can think is, I must have nudged it when I was carrying boxes in or out. Need to be more careful, I guess." The woman's fingers fairly flew as she wrapped floral tape about the stems of callas and roses. "Making a bouquet is like making a larger version of a corsage," she said. "And a corsage is often just three boutonnieres put together. Once you finish the centerpieces, I'll show you how to make the boutonnieres."

Delaney blinked. At the rate she was going with centerpieces, she wouldn't be starting boutonnieres until midnight. She picked up the pace, her mind still mulling over the thermostat issue. "But you've never nudged it before?"

Tina's eyebrows pulled together in confusion.

"The thermostat. You've never nudged it before?"

"No. But I've never been this busy before, either. I had

to prepare for three weddings and a retirement party this weekend." She hot-glued a light blue ribbon around the flower stems she'd just taped. "It was a really inconvenient disaster—as if any disaster is convenient. But a lesson learned about *haste makes waste*." She tied a multi-looped bow and held up the finished bouquet. "I think bouquets look better when the stems are showing, so I always leave them visible under the bottom of the ribbon."

"Gorgeous," Delaney said absently. She couldn't stop thinking about the conversation she'd overheard at last weekend's wedding. Questions were firing in her mind, but she didn't want to come across as a conspiracy theorist. She trimmed some calla lilies and distributed them across several vases, setting up a production line format. "Is it possible someone meant to turn the temperature down a few degrees and accidentally did too much?"

"No one touches the thermostat. It needs to be at forty degrees. No reason to change it."

Delaney allowed herself a tight smile; she'd gotten exactly the answer she needed. She would bet her glass slippers that something wasn't right in Birch Harbor. And she was going to get to the bottom of it. She trimmed more flowers and arranged them in the vases, holding back from saying anything more until she could come up with a non-alarming way to broach the subject now overriding everything else in her mind. Finally, hesitantly, as though the thought had just occurred to her, she asked, "Tina, you don't think someone could have turned the cooler down on purpose, do you?"

Either she was a brilliant investigator or truly delusional.

The woman raised her head, eyes wide. "Why would anyone do that?"

Delaney made a lame gesture with an orchid. "I don't know ... sabotage?" she said weakly. The expression on Tina's face told her that *delusional* was winning.

Tina smiled and her face creased and Delaney felt guilty for even raising the question. She might as well be Godzilla wreaking havoc through the town. But she couldn't stop herself. She had to know. "Is there anyone who might want to ruin your flowers ... or your business? Someone who might turn down the thermostat to do that?"

Tina wrapped a wire around the stems of another bridesmaid's bouquet and didn't respond.

"I'm not accusing anyone," Delaney said hastily. "I've probably just watched too many movies."

"You're sounding a bit like my husband. He wants me to put a lock on the thermostat."

Delaney inhaled softly. Validation. She wasn't so crazy after all. Let Mike laugh at her theory now. "Did anyone new come in the store Wednesday? Anyone acting strangely?" She tried to concentrate on arranging flowers, but it taking all her self-control to keep from begging for the names of all the customers from that day.

Tina stopped to think. "I don't entirely remember who was here. You know how one day blends into the next, especially at my age. I suppose I could check my receipts."

Yes, praise God, let's check the receipts!

Tina went into the office and pulled a stack of papers from a file drawer. She began to flip through them, thinking out loud. "No. No. Not her. Not her, either. Not him—"

"Wait a minute. Tell me who you're talking about. You may be too close to this to be objective."

Tina pursed her lips. "This first one is another bride whose wedding is tomorrow. It surely wouldn't be her." She held up a receipt "And this, this is Robot's Real Estate. They order flowers every week for their open houses." She ran through a couple of other customers who didn't appear to have any connection to the will or Delaney's aunt

"Anyone else?"

"Dan Hobart was in that day."

"Dan?" Surely he wouldn't have tried to undermine her success. Wouldn't make any sense.

"Flowers for his wife. Said they'd finished their birthing classes and he wanted to send her flowers to celebrate. Isn't that sweet?"

Delaney nodded. "Couldn't have been Dan. Anyone else?"

"There's a few more." Tina flipped through the remaining receipts. "Your uncle Joe stopped in."

"My uncle?" Delaney's heart almost stopped beating. Hide in plain sight—or something like that. "What did he want?"

"Ordered a plant to be sent as an anniversary gift." She examined the receipt more closely. "And Claire got a spring bouquet for the office—I made it up on the spot."

Her uncle had opportunity. And motive. Even though she'd thrown his name out to Mike last weekend, she hadn't truly believed he would do anything to undermine her success. He may have always been a loner ... fixated on making money, but she had trouble believing he would be so devious. "Is that it then, for Wednesday? No other customers?"

Tina showed her two other receipts belonging to people who didn't appear to have any connection to Aunt Ellie. "I'm just a small shop, so you see why it's hard for me to believe ... I mean, who of these people would want to hurt my business?"

"I don't know. Maybe you did accidentally nudge the dial." Delaney squeezed her hands into fists. And maybe her uncle knew exactly what he was doing when he came in here that day. Working to get an inheritance.

———

Mike sat forward on the couch and checked the time on his phone. Nine forty-five. Delaney said she'd call when they were done making bouquets; obviously they were still working. He'd talked to her earlier and offered to help, but she assured him everything was in control, no assistance necessary. "This is harder than it looks," she said. "By the time you learn, we'll be done. Besides, I've got to break away to go to the rehearsal."

So here he sat in front of the TV, half watching *The Terminator*. Great movie. Just not what he wanted to be doing right now. He helped himself to a handful of chocolate-covered raisins from the theater-sized box on the couch next to him. Andie was sleeping at a friend's house. Dan and Lauren were at home, hoping labor would begin any minute. And though he knew he could go down to Ollie's Tap and run into any number of acquaintances, he didn't want to.

After last night in the car, what he wanted to do was spend more time with Delaney.

He'd called her, ostensibly to check on how they were doing with the flowers, but the truth was, he wanted to see her—and not as a ploy to make her stay in town to finish the weddings. He tried to convince himself that she might be everything he didn't need, that he might end up feeling like he'd taken one step forward and two back, but he'd made the call anyway.

He slouched into the couch, disinterested in the movie, every now and then reciting one or another of the best-known lines along with the actors. Gradually, exhaustion from their all-night road trip to Chicago took over, and as his defenses dropped and thoughts of Delaney blocked out everything else, he finally succumbed to sleep.

The ringing of his phone jarred him to full consciousness, and he jerked upright in confusion. He glanced at the time before swiping into the call. Ten-thirty? He'd fallen asleep? He stifled a yawn. "Hello?"

"Flowers all done," Delaney said in a cheery voice. "Don't tell me you were sleeping."

"No, no. TV. Just watching TV. Terminator. Um, I mean, the news. You're finished, huh? And the rehearsal? Done? That went okay, too?" He knew he sounded semi-coherent.

"The flowers are beautiful. The rehearsal went fine, totally to plan."

"Busy night."

"And not done yet. I have to run down to the beach to make sure the tent and lights are set up the way they should be, and the chairs and tables have been delivered. I'm not risking any disasters—just want to do a quick check for any obvious issues."

"Not much time in the morning for last-minute inspections," he said.

"Exactly."

There was an enthusiasm in her voice he found really appealing. "You sound awfully energetic after driving all night, working on flowers all day, and coordinating a wedding rehearsal."

"Amazing, isn't it? No. It's because I just had a shower and washed away the fatigue. Presto-change-o, I'm wide awake. Once I sit down, I'll probably fall asleep in seconds. Hope so, anyway." She let out a laugh and the sound slid over him like a soft caress. "Otherwise, I'll be the zombie stumbling around the wedding tomorrow."

"Sounds like an appropriate guest for Bridezilla's special day. Need any help?"

"No, I should be okay. But thanks."

Mike wandered into the kitchen and stared into the refrigerator. He thought about Delaney on the beach, alone in the dark. Of course she'd be okay. She was used to driving her own train. Though, knowing her, she'd stay there half the night fine-tuning things. And if she was going to be on top of her game tomorrow, she really needed to get some sleep. So did he, but that catnap he just finished would keep him awake for hours.

A beer might make him tired. *A beer might make Delaney tired.*

He reached into the refrigerator and pulled out a six-pack of Spotted Cow, hefted it in one hand as he debated the merits of stopping by the beach. Without consciously making a decision, he stuck a bottle opener in his pocket, scooped up his keys from the kitchen table, slipped his feet into flip-flops, and strode out the door.

Ten minutes later, he'd parked at the beach and was heading across the sand, six-pack in one hand and a couple of lap blankets from the trunk in the other. The beam of a flashlight flickered under the big white tent in front of him, and he had fleeting second thoughts. What would Delaney think about him showing up uninvited, a six-pack and blankets in hand?

He slowed his steps. Hell, she could take it all wrong or she could take it in the spirit he was offering it—respite from a long, stressful couple of days. Only one way to find out. He made his way toward the flashlight beam, feet sinking into the soft, still-warm sand.

Suddenly, glaring light hit him full in the face and he put up a hand to shield his eyes. "Hey, it's me," he said.

"Mike! You almost gave me a heart attack! What are you doing out here?" Delaney aimed the light toward the ground and walked toward him, casually dressed in leggings and a T-shirt, her hair tumbling in loose ringlets around her face, still damp from her shower.

He was tempted to drop everything he was holding, take her into his arms right then, and kiss her senseless. "If you're going to be any good tomorrow, you need to call it a day. Figured maybe a beer or two would help you unwind so you can get some sleep."

She smiled at him. "That's so nice. Thanks. Just one more thing I want to check."

He followed her across the beach and tried not to notice her trim butt in those leggings, tried not to wonder whether she had on underpants, because she sure as hell wasn't wearing a bra. He pictured Delaney in the shower, the water running like a silken sheet over her flushed face, her breasts, her belly, her—

He swallowed hard. This was Pumpkin McBride he was having lascivious thoughts about. Pumpy.

No, Pumpy was gone.

Delaney.

Oh, hell.

She shone the flashlight into the woods along the edge of the sand. "This is where the bride is supposed to get on a white horse and ride to the groom. But ever since the rehearsal, I've been thinking we need to start farther back, so no one gets a glimpse of her until she rides into view."

"You had the horse here tonight?"

"No. Just did a walk-through." Holding the light out to illuminate the beach ahead, she pointed toward a bend in the woods along the shore. "There. If she came from back there, it would be better, don't you think?" She looked at him and grinned, and he wanted to run a finger over her beautiful lips and follow it with his mouth.

"Oh yes, much better."

"Okay, okay, I'll quit for the night," she said, laughing. "I'm ready for a beer, even though I still have important things to do tonight."

"Like what?"

"Like iron an outfit for tomorrow. I'll be nervous enough in the morning without having to worry about what to wear."

"Think of how relaxed you'll be ironing with a beer or two in your system. How early is the wedding again?" Mike laid out one of the small blankets and tossed the other in the sand.

Delaney sat cross-legged on the blanket and shut off the flashlight. He settled beside her and waited for his eyes to adjust to the muted light cast by the half moon.

"One o'clock," she said. "But the hospitality service is coming early to set up the bar, the dance floor, the tables, that kind of stuff. And the florist will be here early to decorate the aisle and set up the wedding arbor. I'm meeting everyone about eight."

"Then we won't stay too late, so you can get a decent night's sleep." Mike popped the caps off two bottles, handed one to Delaney, then tapped her beer with his. "To your success in the wedding-planning business."

"Thanks. I'll need it for this all-day affair. Ceremony and pictures. Hors d'oeuvres and champagne. Dinner at four, a band, dancing ... This is a busy wedding." She took a swallow of beer. "I just hope everything comes off okay."

"It will. You're already getting good at it. And you're learning from an expert—your aunt." He brought his bottle to his mouth.

"Speaking of my aunt, you're never going to guess what happened at the florist today. In fact, you'll probably want to apologize for ever doubting me. You may even go so far as to say, *Delaney, you're absolutely brilliant.*"

"I can't wait to hear this."

She recounted the discussion she'd had with Tina about the thermostat. "Guess who was in the shop the day the thermostat got turned down."

He mulled it over for a few seconds. "I don't know. Eliza Doolittle?"

"The flower girl from *My Fair Lady*?" Delaney smacked him on the arm. "I don't think I'll even tell you." She lifted her chin and looked out over the water.

He laughed. "I'm sorry. Tell me. Come on. *Please?*"

She leaned toward him and he could smell the sweet scent of her shampoo.

"My uncle Joe. What do you think of that, Mr. Nonbeliever?"

"Your uncle? Still into that conspiracy theory, huh?" he asked, more to force his brain away from thoughts about Delaney smelling so wonderful and quite possibly *sans* underwear, and less because he cared whether she was into conspiracy theories.

"All I know is that last weekend I overheard someone say that if Storybook Weddings had a few more problems the handwriting would be on the wall. So it seems a bit suspicious that, suddenly, all the flowers were ruined. My uncle had motive. And now we know he had opportunity."

"But he doesn't have *need*. And, I don't think he has the personality for it, either."

Delaney sighed. "Yeah, I know. I hate even thinking this about him."

"You can't discount coincidence. Truth can be stranger than fiction." Mike finished his beer and opened two more, handing one to Delaney.

"But the thermostat got turned down. And the cake got mysteriously canceled."

"And the singer got laryngitis."

"Don't be silly. No one could cause that to happen."

"Exactly. Some things just happen." Mike paused for a

beat. "Okay, let's suppose something underhanded is going on. Did Tina see your uncle go into the cooler?"

"No. But she was so busy she wasn't paying attention. He wouldn't have had to be in there for long." Delaney set her empty bottle into the cardboard holder and took a swallow of the fresh beer.

"So we don't actually know if your uncle had opportunity. I hate to say it, but I don't think there's enough here to mean anything."

Delaney sighed. "Yeah. It felt so good to maybe figure things out."

They stared out at the bay in silence, finishing their second bottle, then opening the last two. Mike didn't know what to believe about her uncle, didn't even want to consider that in the midst of everything else, they might have a saboteur. He inhaled the fresh air, the soothing scent of water and sand, and felt every muscle in his body loosen. Delaney shifted next to him, stretched her legs out in front of her and leaned back on one hand. He could feel the warmth of her leg against his. He tried to concentrate on conspiracy theories, but the only thing he could think of was kissing Delaney. Laying her down in the sand and kissing her.

14

───────

Delaney ran her fingers through her hair to loosen some of the knots caused by the breeze on her wet hair. She savored the cold beer as it slipped down her throat. "I think my problem is a too-active imagination," she said. "Must come from being in advertising."

"Don't tell me all that stuff in commercials isn't true."

"Oh, it's all true, believe me." She snorted out a laugh. "Thanks for coming out here tonight. Who knows how much bigger my mind might have made this conspiracy by tomorrow, otherwise? Besides, this downtime is just what I needed. I'm not sure going back to my wedding-strewn apartment would have done the trick."

The breeze shifted off the lake and the temperature dropped a few degrees. She shivered.

"Cold?" Mike asked.

"Just a little."

He opened the extra blanket and wrapped it around her shoulders, pulling the ends together under her chin. His thumb brushed across her jaw and gently turned her head to face him. In the pale moonlight, his eyes were narrowed and dark. He was looking at her in a way he never had before. Her stomach clenched, goosebumps rose on her arms. He drew her close until their mouths were inches apart, until she could feel his heat.

"I'm not so cold anymore," she chirped, staring at his mouth because she wasn't quite sure what to make of him and determined not to get caught in those eyes again. She knew she should pull back and make a joke about how she was Pumpkin and how different they were from each other and look at what moonlight and a beach could do. Then they would share a laugh and escape this moment. His fingers curled into her hair, caressed the back of her head. She had to say something, anything. She raised her eyes tentatively to his, felt herself begin to sink into their darkness again.

Now. Say something now.

She couldn't form the words. And just when she decided that the way out was to drink more beer and was lifting her bottle, he bent forward to slant his mouth across hers, taking possession of her lips as if he'd owned them for a lifetime.

This was a kiss between lovers. She knew it. He knew it. *And she had a bottle of beer in her hand.*

He deepened the kiss, pulled her against him, his hands cradling her head as he kissed her hard. He tasted of beer, and then he just tasted of Mike and she couldn't get enough of him.

He kissed her throat, trailed kisses over her jaw and she let her head drop back, shivering beneath his touch.

"Lose the bottle," he muttered. "It's cramping our style."

She laughed and tossed it into the sand.

Mike shifted their positions so they were lying on their sides facing each other, their legs entwined, his hands skimming soft skin of her stomach.

She pushed up on one elbow. "What ..." she said as she tried to catch her breath. "What is this all about?"

He rolled to his back and looked at her from beneath heavily lidded eyes. He reached up to cup her cheek with his hand and she leaned into his palm. "I don't exactly know. Do you have to have an explanation?"

She thought a moment, then shrugged. "It's just, I'm Pumpkin ..."

"Honey, you are so far from Pumpkin, I'm about to lose my mind."

She ran her hand down the muscles of his arm. He wrapped her fingers in his, then brought her hand to his mouth and pressed a kiss to her palm. "You are a beautiful, intelligent woman."

He drew a hand over her T-shirt, across her breasts, teased her through the knit fabric until every nerve in her body was engaged. "I can't figure out why it took me so long to figure it out."

He pulled her on top of him and kissed her again. She loved the way his hard body felt against hers, the way his hands touched her, the way she was touching him. "Slow learner," she said matter-of-factly, and he laughed and pulled her shirt up and over her head and rolled her onto her back. He kissed her breasts and slid a hand down her lower back to cup her rear end and pull her tight against him. She could feel his need, mirroring her own. "Although

... maybe I'm wrong about the slow-learner part," she murmured.

He grinned mischievously. "I think you'd be more comfortable with those leggings off."

He slipped his hands beneath the elastic waistband of her sweatpants. And she let him. She gave herself up to his kiss, knowing that if nothing else came of her time as a wedding planner, at least she would know she'd opened and closed every door she'd ever wanted. And if that wasn't enough, well, it would have to be. Because, just like any good business decision, she knew what her options were, she knew what the consequences of each choice were, and she was willing to take the risk associated with this one.

———

Heavy with sleep, Delaney stretched out on her side and let her thoughts drift in the nirvana between unconscious and awake. She couldn't believe how well she'd slept last night. She pulled the fleece blanket over her bare shoulders like a shield against the cool air, and let the soft sounds of the surf lull her to consciousness.

The surf?

She opened one eye to the soft gray early-morning light. A seagull stood not five feet away from her. A seagull in her bedroom?

The bird flapped its wings and flew away, and Delaney opened both eyes, now fully awake. Wait. She wasn't home in her bed—she was on the beach. She'd stayed all night on the beach ...

Oh my God.

She pushed up on one elbow and turned her head. Mike was sleeping on his back next to her, one arm bent over his face, not a sign of tension marring his features.

She'd made love with Mike last night. She cringed, remembering. On the beach. Under the moonlight. They'd rolled around on a blanket in the sand like teenagers until who-knew-when in the morning and then fallen asleep, dead to the world.

And now the sun was up.

She watched Mike's chest rise and fall, and it took everything she had not to touch him, not to lay her mouth on his and wake him with a kiss, not to press her body to his, make love with him again, make him hers.

Make him hers? She knew better than that; *he would never be hers.* No matter how wonderfully relationships began, they never lasted. She had to get out of here. A seagull squawked overhead and she followed its flight with her eyes, watched it land down the beach to fight over something with another gull.

Make him hers? She didn't want that path. What had she been thinking last night? She'd told herself she was opening one door so she could close another, that making love with Mike just this once would allow her to let go of her infatuation. Except ... She looked at Mike and felt an ache behind her breastbone. She hadn't closed the door at all, only left it hanging open, banging in the wind.

She pulled her arm out from under the blanket and checked her watch. Six-fifteen. She needed to get out of here before the joggers and dog walkers started showing up. Before the hospitality-service workers arrived. Before she had to face Mike.

Pressing the blanket to her chest, she picked her clothes out of the sand and gave them a shake, sending granules of sand in every direction. Well, wouldn't these be comfy to wear? Lying on her back, she wriggled into her clothes under the blanket, conscious every moment of Mike's naked body next to her.

She looked at him again. Much as she wanted to escape in silence, she couldn't just leave him here, sleeping. She nudged his shoulder. "Mike! Wake up!"

Yawning, he opened his eyes a crack. "Morning, beautiful," he said sleepily. "What're you doing?" He ran a hand down her arm, and she shivered from his touch.

"We stayed all night." She gestured toward the bay. "It's past six. I have to get out of here before the workers start arriving."

Mike rubbed his eyes and sat up. He tossed back the blanket and reached for his shorts and T-shirt. "All night, huh?"

Delaney's skin tightened at the sight of him completely uncovered. *Get away. Now.* She stood and stepped toward the water to get a better view of where the reception tent had been set up. Though she didn't expect the workers or the florist for more than an hour, it would be just her luck that they'd want to get an early start. Luckily, no one had arrived yet, and the only cars in the parking lot belonged to her and Mike.

She raised her face skyward. The wind was light and the air already warming; it would be a gorgeous day for the wedding. She ran the fingers of one hand through her hair like a comb, then used both hands to try to work out the tangles. Served her right for rolling around on a blanket in the sand with wet hair.

Behind her, Mike laughed. "Hey, Medusa, I think it might be hopeless."

She whirled round and feigned offense. "Medusa?"

"I just call it like I see it." He shook off the blankets and grinned at her, all cute and fresh from sleep, his brown hair falling on his forehead, those blue eyes trying to dance their way into her heart.

She pulled her gaze away. She wasn't going to get sucked into something again, wasn't going to let her emotions get involved when she knew exactly where it would lead. Where it always led. *Nowhere.*

Mike came up beside her, the six-pack of empties in one hand, the blankets in the other. He gave her a puzzled look. "Okay, let's go."

They walked across the beach in silence, every step leading them further away from where they'd been last night—and where they'd gone. She couldn't want him. It was as simple as that. And every step made her more convinced that she was making the right decision.

———

This wasn't exactly how Mike had pictured the morning after. The warm, responsive woman he'd been with last night had completely disappeared. So much for waking in the wee hours and tucking his body around hers, the two of them slipping back to sleep entwined. Maybe Delaney was just jittery about the wedding she had to oversee. He touched her arm. "Hey, don't worry. You'll do great today."

She gave him a tight smile. "I hope so."

"By this time tomorrow, it'll be over. And within a few days, you'll have another satisfactory rating. Two wedding successes down."

They reached the parking lot and stopped at Delaney's silver BMW. "It was fun last night." Mike said.

She nodded and unlocked the car door.

"I'll call you," he said. "Maybe we can take the Chevy out to Sunset Point again."

She shook her head. "It was the beer, Mike. Liquor does that to people." She waved her keys. "And exhaustion. All night driving to Chicago and back. Catching catnaps in the car. You going to work all afternoon. Me doing flowers and the wedding rehearsal. And then there was the moon and the water and the sand. Well, what would you expect? I mean, what would anyone expect?"

He loved how she gestured with her hands when she got agitated. "What are you talking about?"

"Fatigue. It caused the beer to go straight to our heads, released our inhibitions and made us do things we otherwise would never have done." She got into her car and jammed her keys in the ignition.

She believed that?

A big white truck pulled into the lot and parked in a spot near the beach.

"Dammit, there's the hospitality guys," Delaney said. "I knew they'd come early. I knew it. I have to go." She started the engine and put the car into *Reverse* and he jumped back so he wouldn't get run over. "See you later. I'll let you know how the wedding goes."

"Okay. And, Delaney—"

But she was already driving away. He climbed into his SUV and followed her out of the park, replaying in his mind their night on the beach, remembering the woman he'd made love to on a blanket in the sand. Fatigue? No way. What happened between them wasn't about fatigue at all.

15

———

Whenn Delaney returned to the beach an hour later, she found the hospitality staff and the florist already hard at work. She jumped out of her car and smoothed her tan skirt, which she'd quickly ironed as soon as she got home. Despite all the turmoil already this morning, she'd still managed to stick to the original schedule she'd set for herself.

Beneath the reception tent, the tables had been set up and white tablecloths spread. Against this ground, the white calla lily and purple orchid centerpieces looked even more exotic than they had in the florist's shop.

Delaney stepped across the sand toward the rows of chairs that had been arranged facing the bay. Here, beneath the summer sky, the bride and groom would take their vows with the cobalt-blue water of Green Bay as a backdrop. She slowly walked down the aisle, the chairs on either side adorned with the beautiful arrangements she and Tina had made yesterday. Stopping under the wedding arbor, decorated with orchids and callas and roses, suddenly she felt the tremulous anticipation of a soon-to-be bride.

Tina came up the aisle toward her, smiling. "Well? What do you think?"

"It's more beautiful than I imagined it would be," Delaney said.

"You should be proud—without your trip to Chicago, this wouldn't have been possible. Where would you like me to put the bouquets, boutonnieres and corsages? They're still in the van."

"Just put them in my car. I'll run them over to the inn where the bridal party is getting dressed." She handed her keys to Tina, then hurried toward a blue-jeaned man opening the back of a horse trailer.

"Everything ready to go?" she asked.

"Yup. Takin' him down there right now. Rather have him in the fresh air than cooped up in here for the next couple hours." He backed a white horse out of the trailer, the same horse Delaney had watched the bride practice riding.

"I'm going to check on the bridal party, but I'll be back thirty minutes before the ceremony starts," Delaney said. She debated taking him down the beach to discuss tethering the horse around the bend, but decided against it. She didn't want to return to the spot where she and Mike had made love last night. Didn't want to remember what he tasted like. Didn't want to remember what it felt like to have him on top of her. Didn't want to have to keep working at not feeling anything.

As the handler led the horse across the parking lot and onto the sand, she crossed her fingers that everything would come off without a hitch. First, the bridesmaids would come down the aisle, then a duet would sing a shortened version of *The Wedding Song*, followed by the blare of trumpets, the audience would stand, and then the bride in her elegant white gown, would come down the beach riding sidesaddle on the white horse. Everything on cue. Just like in the movies. Too bad she wouldn't have the option of another take if it all went wrong.

She closed her eyes a moment and sent up a prayer for the best. The whole horse thing would fine if the bride was an accomplished rider, but she'd only been on a horse a couple of times—and that was to learn sidesaddle for her wedding. This could turn out to be perfect all right ... for the blooper reel.

Delaney wandered to the edge of the water and watched the shallow waves breaking on the deep blue of the bay. Last night in the darkness, the water had almost seemed black—

No. She wasn't going to do this to herself. Those who failed to remember history were destined to repeat it. And she wasn't going to repeat what her mother had lived.

Thirty minutes later, she carried the box of corsages, boutonnieres, and bouquets into the quaint inn where the bridal party was dressing. The mother of the bride accosted her the moment she stepped through the door. "I'm so glad you're here. My Juliana doesn't like the garter."

Delaney fought to keep her eyes from rolling right up to the ceiling. This job had challenges she'd never realized existed. She made her way to the guest room where the bride was ensconced. "You look beautiful, Juliana. Now, what could be wrong on such a perfect day?" she said in a saccharine-sweet voice.

"The garter is so tight."

"Let me take a look."

Juliana pulled up the hem of her dress to reveal the garter high on her thigh. Delaney choked back a laugh. Was there something about weddings that turned women into imbeciles?

"Oh, oh, the garter's only supposed to be symbolic," she said. "Since it's not holding up hosiery, just pull it down to your knee—even below if you want. It'll be a lot more comfortable."

The bride pulled the garter lower. "Much better."

"What would we do without you?" her mother said.

"What indeed?" Delaney replied in her saccharine voice. Yes, she was getting good at this, if she did say so herself.

She peeked through the slatted window shutter to spot two white limousines pulling into the lot. "The limos are here. It's almost time. Any last concerns or questions about anything? The ceremony? The horse? Anything?"

The bride shook her head.

"Okay, then. Here are the wrist corsages for the mothers and the bouquets for you and the girls. I need to quick pin the boutonnieres on the guys. And then, we'll see you at the beach." She hugged the bride.

Showtime, she said to herself. Damn, she was actually having fun.

An hour later, the bridesmaids were lined up at the beach and ready to go. Delaney was delighted at how beautiful everyone looked, the bridesmaids in their tea-length pastel blue dresses, the groom and groomsmen in sand-colored linen suits with powder-blue dress shirts. As soon as she got the processional started, she took off through the woods to the place where the horse was tethered. Hopefully, the bride was already in the sidesaddle.

As she neared, she could see the handler holding the horse's reins and the bride standing several feet away. Uh-oh. "What's going on?" she asked.

Neither answered. Delaney glanced between the two. "Someone talk. Now."

"I don't think I can do it," the bride said, staring at the horse.

Strains of *The Wedding Song* floated toward them on the breeze. Delaney blew out a breath. Oh God. She should have known this was coming—the girl had practically been falling off the animal during riding practice. "No worries. You don't have to." The saccharine voice came so easily now.

"You don't think everyone will be upset?"

"Not at all. They'll understand." She touched the handler on the elbow. "Don't you agree?"

"I—I don't know ..."

Delaney waved a hand. She had no time for equivocating. "That's because you have a vested interest. Believe me, everyone will get over it."

Trumpets blared. A wave of heat cascaded over Delaney. They needed to get this bride to the aisle.

"That's such a relief." Juliana visibly relaxed. "I don't want Nick to be hurt."

Delaney put an arm around the girl's shoulders.

"Honey, all Nick really cares about is that you become his wife."

Juliana's mother burst out of the trees, puffing. "What's going on?"

"Nothing!" Delaney, the handler and the bride said in unison.

Delaney stepped into the mother's path and the woman neatly sidestepped her and made a beeline for her daughter. "Everyone is waiting. You need to get on that horse and get going." She glared at Delaney. "We're behind schedule."

"I can't do it," Juliana said.

"Do what?"

"Ride the horse," Delaney answered at the same moment Juliana said, "Get married."

Delaney stared at the bride, visions of her inheritance evaporating. "What?"

"I can't get married."

"I thought you couldn't ride the horse!"

"Why wouldn't I be able to ride the horse? I've been practicing. And it's so romantic." She ran a hand down the animal's neck. "I just can't get married."

"This is ridiculous!" her mother cried. "Do you know how much we've spent already? You get on that horse—"

"No."

She turned Delaney. "You tell her. She'll listen to you. Tell her. Everyone feels like this before they get married."

"Everyone feels like this before they get married," Delaney repeated.

"I didn't," the handler said.

"Be quiet," Delaney and the mother told him.

"Go ahead." Juliana's mother waved a hand at Delaney, her bracelets clattering.

Delaney's eyes widened. She was supposed to convince the bride to buy into the myth of happily ever after? *And if she didn't, everyone's inheritance was as good as gone.*

Delaney looked at Juliana and knew she couldn't lie. "Don't do it," she said softly. "Don't do it unless you're sure. Because the odds aren't with you. Every day lots of new marriages begin ... and lots of old ones falter ... and many of them fail."

The mother's face flamed red, but Delaney ignored her. "*They lived happily ever after* is a myth, a fairytale put out there by Snow White and Cinderella and—"

"That's quite enough," the mother snapped.

"—Sleeping Beauty. They all got a prince, but what did they have to give up to get them? And who truly knows how things turned out in the long run?"

"You're fired!" The bride's mother looked apoplectic.

Well, that sealed everyone's inheritance. No reason to stop now. "So if you don't want to get married, don't. Go write your own life's story without this guy."

"Honey, don't listen to her, she's just—"

"Shut up, Mother." Tears welled in Juliana's eyes.

Delaney clenched her teeth. Did she really want to be responsible for this girl not getting married? She took hold of Juliana's arms and dove into uncharted territory. "But if by some chance, some wonderful chance, you're one of the lucky ones who somehow found the man who is your other half, the man without whom the days aren't complete and the nights are empty, you should get down on your knees in gratitude. And then you should marry him."

The maid of honor broke out of the woods, her expression frantic. "What is going on? The trumpets played. And now the duet is singing a song that isn't even in the program."

"Take my mother back to the wedding," Juliana said.

"That's it? You want me to go out there and tell everyone it's off?" Her mother put a hand to her forehead. "I need an aspirin."

"It's off?" The maid of honor's mouth dropped open.

Juliana looked at Delaney for a very long moment. Then she said, "I can't even imagine my life without him."

Another hopeless romantic. Delaney was almost beginning to envy their foolish optimism.

The bride turned to the handler. "I'm ready. Let's go." He helped her onto the horse. She straightened her beaded white dress and smiled down at them. "Get to your places, everyone. I'm getting married today ... and we're late."

———

"You want to go hit some balls at the playground?" Dan stood on Mike's front stoop, baseball glove on his left hand and a cap backward on his head.

It felt like they were twelve years old again.

"Where's your wife and son?"

"Kristian's napping. Lauren's washing the kitchen floor. Kicked me out of the house. Said she's nesting. And that I'm hovering and driving her nuts and she'll call if she goes into labor."

"Sounds to me like she's trying to get labor started."

"Yep. So you want to play?" Dan stepped into the house.

"Yeah, I'll come." Mike turned and yelled down the hall, "Hey, Andie, you want to hit some balls at the playground?"

His daughter rounded the corner from the kitchen and gave him two thumbs-up. They grabbed baseball gloves, a metal bat, and some balls from the garage, then headed toward the nearby schoolyard.

"It's almost summer vacation!" Andie sang, skipping ahead of them on the sidewalk in shorts and running shoes. "Seven more days of school!" Half a block up, she spun and ran back to throw herself into Mike's arms. "Love you!"

"I love you, too." He laughed.

She fell into step beside him and clasped his hand. "So where were you last night?"

He blinked. She'd slept at a friend's house; how did she know he hadn't come home? "Home."

"Then how come when you picked me up this morning you had on the same clothes as yesterday?"

Dan cleared his throat.

"Because they were ... handy. Right on the floor. And it's Saturday. And since when did you start caring what I wear, anyway?"

Andie shrugged and ran ahead of them again.

"You're wearing the same clothes as yesterday?" Dan looked at him sideways. "Sounds suspicious to me, too."

Mike threw him a warning look. "I'm showered and changed now."

"Hmm, seems like there might be a story in there somewhere," Dan muttered.

Andie raced back toward them. "Rock, paper, scissors to see who hits first!"

By the time they reached the schoolyard, the major decisions had all been made: Mike was hitting, Dan was pitching, and Andie was covering the outfield. As she jogged out to center field, Dan turned to Mike and asked, "So, what'd you do last night?"

"Helped Delaney." Mike tossed the extra balls toward the pitcher's mound.

"Delaney?" Dan drew her name out slowly. "You mean *Pumpkin?*"

"No. I mean Delaney."

"Ohh. I sense a shift of some sort. Let me think about this." Dan picked up the bat and took a couple of practice swings. "She doesn't have a job to go back to, so you no longer have to romance her to keep her in town. But you're spending time with her, anyway. What could this mean? Did someone hit a single last night?"

"It means nothing."

"The hell it doesn't." Dan handed over the bat and headed out to the pitcher's mound. "That's okay," he said over his shoulder. "I've got the rest of the afternoon to get it out of you." He positioned himself in a pitcher's stance, then lobbed a ball toward Mike who let it fly past to crash into the backstop fence.

"Stee-rike," Dan called out.

"Ball one," Mike said. "That was so low, if I hit it I'd be golfing."

"Let's see. You both went to Chicago. Then you went to work on Friday and Delaney went to the florist's. So, where'd you help her last night?" Dan called as he let the next pitch fly.

Mike hit a line drive up the first base side and Andie chased it into the outfield. "At the beach."

"The beach." Dan began to chortle. "Timing submarine races?"

"Setting up for the wedding."

Andie ran toward Dan and tossed him the ball underhand. He threw another pitch and Mike popped up to center-field, sending Andie running again.

"What's to set up? That's for the rental company to do." Mike shrugged.

Dan came toward him waving his glove. "Spill it. What were you doing at the beach?" he asked in a low voice even though Andie was on the other side of the field. "*Pumpkin?*"

"Don't be crude."

A shout from Andie drew their attention. She hefted the ball and it hit the ground twenty feet away.

Dan grinned. "Wow. I'm right, aren't I? Pumpkin McBride. You were doing Pumpkin."

"If you open your mouth, or in any way let her know that you know, I will put you permanently in the trunk of Ellie's old Chevy."

Dan held up both hands in surrender. "You know me. No secrets ever escape these lips."

"I mean it. You open your mouth and I'll kill you."

"Okay, okay, okay. Don't worry. Hey, I'm glad for you."

"I don't know. She's leaving town in two months."

"So?"

"Hit the ball!" Andie yelled from the outfield. "Two more at bats! Then I'm up!"

"Keep your pants on!" Mike yelled back. He looked at Dan. "And don't forget, I have Andie to consider."

At the next pitch, Mike hit a solid grounder deep into left field. As Andie chased it down, Dan jogged toward him again. "Why would Andie have to know about it?"

"Are you kidding? Andie seems to know everything that goes on in this town. Somehow she'd find out. I don't want her to get attached to Delaney and then hurt when she goes back to Boston." And she was going back, of that he was certain.

"Yeah, but isn't Andie helping out at Storybook Weddings after school?"

Mike nodded. "Delaney's just her boss there. Not a woman her father's involved with."

"You're splitting hairs. Andie's already attached to her. She talks about Pumpkin—Delaney—all the time."

"All the more reason for me not to get involved. It's not a good idea." Mike stuck the barrel end of the bat on the ground, leaned on the knob end, and decided to change the subject. "Hey, but here's something that might be important. Ellie's brother was at the florist's the day the thermostat got turned down and all the flowers froze."

"So, the conspiracy returns."

Dan's phone rang and he pulled it from his back pocket. "Hi, hon." He paused. "Are you kidding? I just left. Okay, I'm on my way. Yeah. No. I'll be right there. Don't do anything." Another pause. "*I won't get in an accident.*" He ended the call and slapped Mike on the shoulder. "Guess what?"

"She's in labor."

Dan nodded. "Her water just broke. And her folks are

down in DePere. Can you and Andie babysit Kristian until they get back? Hour and a half?"

"No problem." Mike waved Andie in. "Hey, kid! Lauren's going to have the baby. You want to babysit Kristian a while?"

16

Dusk fell, and Mike wandered outside to sit in one of the chairs on his backyard deck. Lauren's parents had relieved him of babysitting duties hours ago, and now there was just the waiting to be done. He'd always heard second babies came faster than the first, but knowing that didn't do much to speed the time.

He considered swinging by the wedding to see Delaney, but couldn't think of a good reason to go there other than wanting to make sure everything had gone well. Seemed like a weak excuse considering his only connection to the wedding was the will.

He leaned back in the chair and closed his eyes. Maybe he would just sit here a while and think about ... stuff. His marriage. His ex-wife. His daughter. His life. His goals and dreams. New babies. Love.

Delaney.

Naked and soft and hot.

His eyes popped open.

Andie charged out the back door with her friend

Brittany. "Hey, Dad, can I go over to Britty's and roast marshmallows and make s'mores? Did Dan call yet? Did Lauren have a baby?"

"No baby yet, as far as I know. And, yeah, you can go to Britty's. I'm probably going over to the wedding for a while, make sure everything's going okay for Delaney. I won't be gone long. Call me before—"

"Okay, see you later." Andie and Britty raced around the side of the house toward the front yard.

"—you come home." It was nice to see her so happy. She hardly put up a fuss about doing her homework anymore and Delaney was the reason. She wouldn't let Andie do anything in the shop until she'd first completed at least half an hour of homework. More often than not, by the time he picked up Andie, she had her homework done for the night.

He studied the golden-hued sky and considered what Delaney had told him about Joe Waverly and the flower shop. Given the conversation Delaney overheard and the number of oddball things that had gone wrong with this wedding, it might be smart to monitor the next wedding more closely. Keep the names of the vendors close to the vest and maybe float some false vendor names as a diversion. Then see if disaster struck any of them. Might put a spotlight on the guilty party—if there really was one.

He nodded to himself. Not a bad plan. He should probably share it with Delaney. *Right away*. Besides, she'd surely want to know that Lauren was in labor.

———

From the end of the service drive, Delaney watched the wedding guests uninhibitedly dancing on the portable wooden floor that had been laid under the white tent. The horse hadn't thrown the bride. The marriage ceremony was over. The dinner had gone off without a hitch. The band was playing the world's best dance songs. The mother had apologized and rehired Delaney. All was right with the world.

Well, at least with the world of weddings. Her personal life, now that was another story.

She felt a hand on her arm and turned. *Mike.* Her stomach flopped. "What are you doing here?"

"Lauren's in labor."

Delaney gasped. "She is?"

He nodded. "They're at the hospital. Lauren's parents are watching Kristian. And Andie's gone to a friend's house …"

"So you decided to come to the wedding of someone you don't even know?" she teased.

"After everything we've been through the past few days, I kind of feel like I know them."

"Apparently we didn't know them well enough. The bride almost changed her mind at the last minute."

Surprise widened his eyes. "Seriously? What happened?"

"I convinced her that happy endings were possible."

Mike looked up at the sky and Delaney followed his gaze. "What are you doing?" she asked.

"Getting ready for a lightning bolt," he said.

"Very funny. She believed me and that's all that matters." She paused a beat. "So, Lauren's in the hospital?"

For a moment she wondered what it would be like to have a baby, a child to raise, to love. And a husband to share all that with.

"Dan said he'd call as soon as there was any news."

"I'd send her a text, but that's probably the last thing she needs right now."

The band broke into a slow song, soft and romantic, and people paired off on the dance floor. As she watched the couples, an unfamiliar ache squeezed her heart. Babies, husbands, romance. Good God, what was the matter with her these days?

Mike leaned toward her until their shoulders touched. "Want to dance?" he asked.

Them? Here? Now? She shook her head.

"Come on. A celebration dance. You succeeded against the odds once again."

No. Maybe for him it would be a celebration dance. But for her, it would be a reminder that she'd made yet another stupid decision where a man was concerned. "I ... have to work."

"No one needs you right now. Come on."

"We're in a driveway."

"Dance as if no one's watching," he said quietly, channeling James Dean. He took her hand, gave it a gentle tug and she moved into his arms. As the music washed over them on the soft night breeze, they began to dance so slowly their feet were barely moving on the asphalt drive. *Dance as if no one's watching,* her mind whispered before finishing the quote: *Love as if it's all you know.*

Anticipation skimmed through her, and she gave in to the rush of feelings she'd been trying to keep at bay.

Maybe her mother had done it all wrong. Maybe it had been her mother's own fault that nothing worked out. Maybe Delaney wasn't destined to repeat her mother's mistakes. Could it be that, just this once, all the pieces had come together at just the right time?

"I have an idea," Mike murmured.

She pulled back to look up at him, at those eyes that had held her heart for so long, and for the briefest moment was tempted to bare her soul and say, *That we should make love in the sand again?*

———

Mike looked into Delaney's wide hazel eyes, at her lips slightly parted, and couldn't dislodge the image of her beneath him, naked, her red hair tousled like Medusa.

"I have an idea ... about the conspiracy theory," he said, trying to keep his voice steady. "If you're right, if someone is in fact trying to keep you from succeeding ..."

Chicken, he said to himself. The idea he'd been referring to had nothing to do with the conspiracy—and everything to do with a repeat of last night. But he'd pulled back, afraid to push Delaney too hard.

She blinked. Twice. "Oh, right ... you mean my uncle?"

"Or someone. I'm not convinced he's involved."

"Yeah, I know. But he's the only person with motive. So far anyway."

The sounds of the wedding washed over them, happy voices and laughter, the band playing the love song they were dancing to. Mike wanted to run his fingers through Delaney's red hair, tip her head back, and kiss her. Instead, he found himself stuck in what amounted to a business meeting—and he had no one but himself to blame. "First, we have to figure out if someone really is trying to sabotage the weddings," he said. "And if that answer is *yes,* then we need to flush out the culprit."

The song ended, and Delaney immediately stepped out of his arms. "How?"

Mike shrugged. "False information? Maybe feed it to anyone who could have motive. Then wait and watch."

"You mean, like, spread around the name of a different baker than the one we're actually using and wait to see if his oven explodes?"

Mike snorted out a laugh. "Something like that."

"I like that we'd be proactive. As unimaginative as your idea sounds—"

"Unimaginative?" He put a hand over his heart as though mortally wounded.

"Unimaginative, stereotypical, theatrical." She smiled. "But I've been really working hard at these weddings. If someone is causing my stumbles, I want to expose them." She glanced at the reception tent. "I'd better get back. I'm still on duty, and God knows what could go wrong next."

She started across the beach and Mike fell into step next to her. "Hey, about last night," he said. "I didn't come down to the beach expecting—"

"I know that. Sometimes things just happen," she said briskly, waving a hand dismissively. "Circumstances. Happenstance. Doesn't mean anything. Certainly nothing with long-term ramifications."

Delaney sounded like she'd already performed a business analysis of the situation and decided against making an investment. He'd reached the same conclusion this afternoon, but the fact that she kept jumping naked into his mind had made him veer off that course. "Let's just put it behind us," he said.

"Pretend it never happened. Go back to being friends."

"Getting our will requirements completed," he added.

"Absolutely."

He looked over at her, but she kept her eyes straight ahead. Damn, she was beautiful. "Before we do that, though, I need to make one thing clear. It wasn't fatigue."

She turned. "What?"

"It wasn't the fatigue. And it wasn't the beer and the moon and the waves and the sand."

She stared at him a long moment, then shrugged. "Believe what you want," she said in a brittle voice. "I know better."

Mike's phone vibrated and he pulled it out. "It's Dan. You know what that means." He swiped into the call and asked, "Is it safe to say congratulations, yet?"

17

Delaney walked with Mike down the quiet hallway of the hospital maternity ward. *A baby boy*. Lauren and Dan had another son.

The door to Lauren's room was ajar and Mike tapped lightly before pushing it open and stepping inside. Delaney paused in the doorway. Soft afternoon light filtered through the window casting a warm glow on Dan in the rocking chair, the new baby in his arms, swaddled in a blanket. Lauren stood beside him in a pale pink robe, head bent next to his as they watched their new baby sleep.

A sigh caught in Delaney's throat.

"Hey, guys," Mike said quietly. "Congratulations."

Delaney crossed the room to hand their gift to Lauren and gave her a hug. She took a quick peek at the baby. "Sebastian. I love that name. He's beautiful."

"Looks just like his brother," Mike said.

"Yeah." Dan grinned. "My folks were just here with Kristian and he's really excited to be a big brother. We're hoping Sebastian has a little less energy."

Mike held up both hands. "Hate to tell you, but Kristian will teach him everything he knows, so it's a lost cause. Just ask my brother." He sat on the edge of the bed and Delaney joined him.

Lauren lowered herself into the overstuffed easy chair in the corner. "How'd the wedding go last night?" She raised hopeful eyebrows at Delaney.

"Success! Wedding number two is out of the way."

"Everything went great once Delaney convinced the bride to get married," Mike said with a grin.

Dan lifted his gaze from the new baby and planted it firmly on Mike. "You were there, too?"

"He came later," Delaney said quickly. "To discuss setting up a sting before the next wedding."

"So, you've bought into the conspiracy theory now?" Dan looked a bit confused.

"Well, uh, no ... yeah ... It just seems like something might be going on. I'm not convinced Joe Waverly is guilty ... just thought we could try something, see if we flush anyone out."

Dan laughed out loud.

Delaney frowned at him. "We're just going to put out some false information, like, we say we're using a different bakery than the one we actually hired ... and then see if anything goes wrong at the fake bakery. Information gathering is smart business."

Dan let out a snort. The baby stirred and opened his eyes a crack and all four adults froze until he dropped back to sleep.

"I think it's brilliant," Lauren said.

"How will this catch the thief, so to speak?" Dan asked.

"Let's say the baker's oven quits working. There's no proof a person, let alone Joe Waverly, is responsible."

"Got a better idea?" Mike crossed his arms over his chest.

"We've had three suspicious incidents already. Why wait for six to take action? If we're wrong, then all we've wasted is some talk," Delaney pointed out.

The baby stirred again. Lauren took him from Dan and nuzzled her cheek against his forehead. Then she gently laid him in Mike's arms.

He smiled at the baby. "Hey there, Seebass, glad you finally made it." He brushed his thumb against the baby's cheek and cradled him close to his body. Sebastian let out a tiny sigh and settled back to sleep.

Delaney envied the ease with which he held the baby, and then a thought burst into her head with such clarity she almost gasped—if only this were their child he was holding.

"The baby had to be footprinted for his birth certificate." Lauren sipped at the straw in her disposable cup. "Then, they had to get the ink off so his foot wasn't stained."

All three looked at her, trying to follow her train of thought.

"It doesn't hurt him, hon," Dan said.

Lauren rolled her eyes. "I'm thinking about the ink. On cop shows, they put this invisible powder on the doorknobs or the lock to the safe. And when someone tries to break in, the powder stains their hands and won't wash off."

"Sebastian," Mike whispered to the baby, "I think your mama wants to be a private detective. She's worse than I am."

"Think about it. How better to ID the perp?" Lauren asked.

"ID the perp?" Dan echoed incredulously.

"Maybe she's onto something." Delaney gestured at Mike and Dan. "Do you guys know a cop?"

"Sure," Dan said. "It's a small town. But if we ask about something as dumb as this, we're going to have to spill what we're up to and—"

"Where the hell would we use it, anyway? It's not like we're protecting a treasure that's locked up." Mike drew a hand gently over the baby's head and was rewarded with an angry squawk. He threw a panicked look at Lauren. "Sorry."

"Not your fault. He's probably hungry." She nodded at Delaney. "You want to quick hold him before he wakes up?"

"I ... uh ..." Oh, God, she wasn't even sure she knew how. What if she let his neck fall backward? Or touched that soft spot on the top of his head? She had no experience with babies. Before she could articulate an excuse, Mike had gently placed Sebastian in her arms. She held him gingerly, as she'd held every baby that had been thrust at her over the years.

"Couldn't we put that powder on the thermostat at the florist and see if anyone ends up with colorful fingers?" Lauren asked.

Dan shook his head. "Only an idiot would do the same thing twice."

"Never say never." Lauren grinned at her husband. "I don't think the saboteur is going to be a rocket scientist."

"Okay, spymasters," Mike said. "Assume we figure out

where to put this stuff so it gets on the bad guy's fingers. Where are we going to get it?"

"Online," Delaney and Lauren said simultaneously.

"You three are beginning to scare me." Dan looked at his wife. "Lauren, where did you learn this stuff?"

"Knock, knock," a woman's voice said from the doorway.

They all quit talking like guilty teenagers planning to sneak out of the house in the middle of the night.

Joe, Claire, and a stuffed black bear came into the room. "We'll only stay a minute," Joe said. "We heard at church this morning that the little one arrived and we had this gift all ready."

"Oh, look at him!" Claire cried.

The two bent toward the child and Delaney felt a surge of protectiveness.

"He's beautiful." Claire ran a finger gently down the baby's cheek. "So sweet." She handed the stuffed bear to Lauren who ran her hands over the fur. "It's faux mink," Claire said, "but it feels like the real thing."

Delaney touched the downy hair on Sebastian's head and inhaled the soft scents of lotion and powder. The baby opened his eyes and stared up at her, then pursed his lips and made a squeak before closing his eyes again. She cradled him close and touched her lips to the tender skin of his forehead.

"Delaney? Are you listening?" Mike asked.

She looked up. "Oh, sorry. Did I miss something?"

Everyone laughed.

"Babies do that to you," Lauren said.

She nodded, surprised it was happening to her. Now

she understood why fairytales were created. Because, for these flawless, helpless little beings, all you wanted was to ensure happily ever after. Even if you knew it was impossible to deliver.

"We were talking about the weddings," Lauren said. "Don't forget to check with the manager of Harris House about the sprinkler system."

What? Delaney squinted at her.

"Where the wedding is this weekend," Lauren added helpfully.

Of course she knew the wedding was at Harris House. The grounds of that early 20th century manor were so beautifully landscaped, so perfect for weddings, they had to be booked more than a year in advance. But why would Lauren bring it up now?

She glanced at Joe and Claire. Unless ... maybe it had something to do with their earlier conversation about planting false information. "Remind me again what I'm checking on? There are so many details, I start to lose track."

"They've actually forgotten to change the timer on the sprinklers before an event and the system has gone off at the worst times." Lauren waved a hand. "Drenching the guests."

"Seriously?" Delaney asked, not sure whether Lauren was speaking the truth or merely acting for Joe's sake.

"I've never heard anything like this," Claire said.

Lauren nodded. "It's true. Dan used to mow the lawn there in high school and it happened, didn't it, Dan?"

"Couple of times, yeah. Picture the entire wedding party looking like they're in a wet T-shirt contest," he said.

"Come to think of it, maybe you should let the sprinklers go off."

"Daniel," his wife warned.

"I'll talk to the groundskeeper," Delaney said, still trying to figure out if this discussion was reality or a ruse.

"Maybe you should check the timer yourself," Mike said. "Do you know how to set one?"

She shook her head. "All I have to find is the on/off switch. I'm not going to set the thing—just shut it off." The baby's eyes opened, closed, and opened again. "Lauren, he's really starting to wake up."

Lauren slid out of her chair. "It's been three hours since he ate."

"You're probably better off letting management fool with the timer," Joe said. "So nothing gets out of whack."

Delaney shrugged. "Yeah, but I'll check it just in case. Better safe than sorry. Do you know where it is, Dan? In an outbuilding somewhere?"

"It's on the outside wall of the carriage house. Gray box. You can't miss it."

Sebastian began to fuss in Delaney's arms. "I think it's time. This boy needs to eat," she said, handing him back to Lauren.

"We'll be on our way, then," Claire said.

"Congratulations to you both," Joe added.

Delaney shut the door firmly behind them. "That was a setup, right? But was it true? Have the sprinklers gone off during events?"

Lauren let out a laugh. "No. It was all I could come up with on the spur of the moment."

"Good lie," Mike said. "I was impressed. I think Joe and Claire bought it."

"Good. So now you guys take over and flush Joe out. Put some on the timer, then watch the color of his fingers."

"But we don't know that it's Joe," Mike said. "We don't actually know if it's anyone. I think detection powder should be a last-resort thing."

"You think?" Dan made a face.

"Hey, it's a good—" Lauren began, but stopped when Sebastian began to fuss in earnest.

"We'll get out of here, too." Mike pulled open the door and stepped into the hall.

Delaney stopped at the threshold to look back at Dan and Lauren. "Congratulations. You did great." A lump rose in her throat and she swallowed it down. For the first time in as long as she could remember, she was truly envious of a relationship.

18

———

The bells jangled as the door banged against the opposite wall. "Ms. McBride!" someone called from the front of the store.

Delaney scribbled *masking tape* on her shopping list. "Back here!" was all she got out before the owner of Eleganza Cucina, the caterer for the upcoming wedding, sashayed into the back room.

"I have terrible news. Terrible. They shut me down," the woman said, a slight Italian accent evident in her voice.

"Shut what down?"

"My business."

Delaney felt the stirrings of panic. Not another disaster. "Hold on, Annalisa. What are you talking about?"

"A visitor came today from the Department of Health." She waved her hands expressively. "A surprise inspection. They got an anonymous call. And they shut me down."

"How can they shut you down? You have a wedding to cater this weekend."

"I told him that. He said I had an unlicensed facility."

"Do you?" Delaney couldn't believe this was happening.

"Well, no, I didn't think so. But, yes, after talking to him, I guess I do. I cook out of my home."

Delaney didn't even want to ask the next question because she dreaded hearing the answer. "Can you get your home licensed before Saturday?"

"Oh my, no. He said in order for me to do that—" Annalisa composed herself "—I would have to get commercial ovens and refrigerators, a fire-prevention system, attend safety and management courses—"

"That's enough." Delaney held up a hand. The muscles at the back of her neck felt like steel cords. "How could you not have known this?" Anger and frustration were showing in her voice and she didn't care.

"I'm new to catering."

"You've never done this before?"

"Not cooking. *Catering.*" Annalisa splayed a hand across on her chest. "I am a *chef.* I cook at other people's homes. For dinners. Events. The bride's parents have hired me many times before. So when they asked, could I do the wedding, I never even thought about licensing."

Delaney massaged the back of her neck. "Let me get this straight. If this wedding was in someone's house and you cooked in their kitchen, it would be okay."

"Yes."

"But because you're going to cook at home and move the food somewhere else, your kitchen has to be licensed?"

Annalisa nodded.

"This may sound overly simplistic, but can't you just cook everything at the reception site?"

"Harris House?" Annalisa shook her head. "They quit building it during the depression. When they finally finished it, they turned it into a museum. It only has a sink, warming ovens and a refrigerator. It's for staging food, not cooking."

Delaney sighed. "What would happen if you cooked everything at home, anyway?" She knew breaking the law wasn't the answer, but desperation could make criminals out of saints.

"He said if I didn't *cease operations immediately* they'd bring me in front of a judge. Gave me a verbal warning to shut down and said a follow-up letter would come in the mail."

Delaney paced across the room. "So where does this leave us?"

"I need a licensed kitchen to cook in—or you have to find another caterer."

"Before this weekend? It's June! This is one of the busiest wedding weekends of the year. The best caterers are booked a year out." She exhaled sharply. "Do you know anyone with a licensed kitchen you can use?"

Annalisa shook her head again. "Other caterers will need their kitchens Saturday. Like you say, it's the big wedding month. Restaurants—they need their kitchens, too, to cook for their customers. Maybe a school or a church would help. But it's such short notice. I can make some calls ..." She pulled out her phone.

That was pretty much the answer Delaney had expected. "Okay. Let me know if you come up with anything. There's got to be an answer."

As soon as the door closed behind Annalisa, Delaney

slammed her hand against the desk. There was no longer any doubt in her mind that someone was behind this. And as much as it pained her to think it, her uncle was the most likely culprit. He really was the only person who had motive.

Damn, but she'd probably never be able to find a licensed kitchen for this weekend. And as for finding another caterer, well ... the bride was having a turn-of-the-century formal garden reception with a very unusual menu. Delaney might be able to find someone willing to cook but it wouldn't be what the bride ordered. Or if it was, no way would it be made correctly.

Goodbye, inheritance.

She called Mike's law office and started talking the second he picked up the phone. "The wedding saboteur has struck again. The Department of Health just shut down the caterer for Saturday's wedding." She explained the whole story. "*Someone* knew her home wasn't licensed."

"That greedy son of a bitch," Mike said.

"Glad to know we're on the same page."

"Why don't you call the inspector and see if he got a name?"

Delaney tapped a finger on her desk. "He told Annalisa he got an anonymous call. So whoever it was made sure they were covering their tracks."

By the end of the call, Mike was a true conspiracy-theory believer, and Delaney was so dejected she sat at her desk and did absolutely nothing for the next twenty minutes. If her uncle wanted the money so badly, let him have it.

The thought triggered a rebellion in her brain. No way. She wasn't going down without a fight.

She brought up the Google search screen on the computer, reached into the desk drawer to get her aunt's business card file, and started to make calls. Over the course of the next two hours, she learned that none of the church or school kitchens were an option—either they were already booked or had a policy against renting out their kitchens. As for caterers, she'd found just one available—*Millie's Marvelous Meals.*

Delaney looked at Millie's business card again. She drew a slow breath and exhaled. What choice did she have?

Swallowing hard, she called Millie back to provide the full details. "As I mentioned before, the ingredients have all been ordered. They just need to be prepared."

Millie squeaked out a laugh. "I've never made lobster-stuffed filet mignon before. I usually do simpler meals. But I'm willing to try." She managed to sound apologetic and hopeful at the same time.

Willing to try. Delaney could almost hear the bride screeching at dinner, could almost see the big red F on the evaluation form.

"I'll go on online and see what I can find out about making those dishes before this weekend," Millie added.

Marvelous. That made her feel so much better. Delaney could only imagine what would happen to the eggplant rollatini; the grilled new potatoes with baby onions; the mushrooms stuffed with escargot, goat cheese, and caramelized onions.

She gave herself a mental slap. At least she'd found a cook. And at least this woman was willing to *try* to learn how to prepare the food correctly. Maybe Annalisa could assist with the preparation, or even— "It just occurred to me," she said. "Since you've never made these dishes before and time is so tight ... How would you feel about renting your kitchen to Annalisa for the day?"

There was a long pause. "My kitchen?"

"Yes."

"I am the chef in my kitchen."

"I understand, but I just thought that maybe it might make everything simpler all around."

The silence that greeted her sentence dragged on for so long Delaney thought Millie had hung up. "Uh, Millie, you there?"

"I don't rent out my kitchen. I don't know any chefs who do. If you want *me* to prepare this meal, I would be glad to. I'll do my best to make it memorable."

"Oh, that's fine, just wanted to toss it out there. I'm sure it will be. Memorable." Memorable would probably be the nicest adjective she could use to describe this wedding once it was over. All her other choices would, no doubt, involve curse words.

With nothing to lose, she decided to shoot for Plan B. "What about the possibility of Annalisa assisting you with the preparation? If this wedding dinner is successful, it could be a real boon for both of you. But a failure ... well, you know how word gets around."

"I see what you mean. I don't usually share my kitchen, but ... it might help to have Annalisa here, the two of us working together. We could split payment for the job."

"I'm sure she'd be fine with that."

"Okay, that's what we'll do. Can you have her call me?"

By the time they hung up, Delaney could feel a headache trying to develop. She pressed her fingers into her forehead, then rubbed her temples. Another crisis. This wedding planning was going to do her in, in ways the advertising world had never even thought of. She went to the shop entrance to scoop the mail off the floor beneath the mail slot—bills, bills, and more bills, all forwarded from the post office in Boston.

Passing the shelves of white accessories, she reached out to touch the tiara and veil Lauren had plopped on her head the day she arrived. She'd known the job would be hard when she got here, just hadn't realized how hard. Tears pricked the back of her eyes. She wanted to see Mike, wanted him to put his arms around her and kiss her and take her back to the faraway place on the beach where problems didn't seem to exist. At least not until the sun came up.

Yeah, right. Just another daydream that could never come true.

She retrieved her shopping list from the desk, and stuck a note on the door saying she'd gone to the hardware store and would be back soon. As she stepped over the threshold, she gave the doorknob a quick tug to slam the door shut behind her.

As she strode down the sidewalk, the fresh air and sunshine began to lift her mood—and replenish her determination. She *would* get this inheritance. They all would. The more her uncle—or whoever—worked against her, the harder she would work to make sure it was he who failed and not her.

19

Mike grabbed Delaney by the arm and pulled her into the plumbing supplies aisle. He grinned at the surprise that flitted across her face. This was going to be fun. "I got it," he whispered.

She looked at him in confusion. "Got what? And what are you doing here?"

"Hunting for you."

"At the hardware store? There's no privacy in this town," she said without animosity.

"You left a note on your door."

She shrugged. "So what'd you get? The flu?"

He leaned close to her ear. "Detection powder. Violet. I ordered it online."

"You mean the stuff Lauren was talking about?" she practically screeched.

"Shush." He nodded, feeling a little like the kid who'd just discovered where the Christmas candy was stashed.

"You've got to be kidding me! I thought you said it was a last resort."

"I think the caterer being shut down constitutes last resort. I called SpyWizard.com as soon as I got off the phone with you. Got the powder, got an application brush. Everything will be here tomorrow—overnight delivery. Then we just dust the sprinkler timer and wait for your uncle to touch it. If he's behind the problems you've been having, we'll know soon enough."

"Can he wash it off?"

Mike shook his head. "Nothing takes it off—not water, not acetone, not alcohol. He'll have purple fingers for days, and no way to lie his way out of it."

"And you don't think just confronting him might get us the same information without having to go through all this?"

Mike rolled his eyes.

"Just thought I'd ask. But won't he notice purple powder on the timer?"

"It's silver-gray when it goes on—almost the same color as the timer box. It only turns purple when it mixes with skin oils." Mike started to laugh. "The guy said that if the person tries to wash it off with water, the stain will spread."

A customer stopped nearby to examine a showerhead, and Mike took Delaney's hand and tugged her into the next aisle. He regretted not taking her concerns about her uncle more seriously when she first voiced them. "By the way, Dan's on board, too. I told him about the caterer and he agrees, too many coincidences."

"Now I know it must be serious. But have you considered that maybe Uncle Joe didn't fall for Lauren's story?" Delaney asked. "It did sound a bit far-fetched. Besides, he could find out if it's true just by asking the grounds manager."

Mike put a hand on her shoulder and leaned close to her ear. Tried not to let the smell of her shampoo distract him. "He's not going to check it out. Because he can't risk anyone remembering that he was asking questions about the sprinkler system going off during events and then connecting him to the problem later."

"But there'll never be a problem, because we'll make absolutely sure the sprinklers are shut off."

"He doesn't know that."

Delaney frowned.

"What's the matter? I would think you, of all people, would be excited to do this."

She glanced up at him. "What if someone else, a legitimate person, does something with the timer and gets purple fingers, so they wipe the timer off. And there isn't any powder on the timer when the bad guy shows up and then we think the wrong person is guilty."

"God, that's a stretch." He couldn't believe she was balking. "First, I doubt that would happen. But if it does, their fingers won't turn purple right away. So they won't know the purple came from the timer, so they can't wipe it off. And second ..."

She stepped away from him and raised her eyebrows. "Yes?"

He wanted to kiss the doubt off her face. "Second, what have we got to lose?"

She looked up at the ceiling and shook her head. "Nothing. We've got nothing to lose. You're right. Okay, I'm in."

"Great. What are you doing tomorrow night?"

"I thought I'd wash my hair."

"Can it. We've got a mission."

———

The phone rang early the next morning, waking Delaney from a sound sleep. Why, on the one day she decided to sleep in, after a stressful day solving problems in the wonderful, *wacky* world of weddings, did her phone have to ring at the crack of dawn?

She fumbled about on the nightstand until her fingers closed over her phone. As she swiped it open, her brain registered a Boston area code, and she wished she'd looked at the number more closely before answering. The last thing she needed was to talk to bill collectors—although she didn't think things had gotten that bad for her yet. "Hello?" she croaked.

"Delaney! Good morning," a man said.

She lay back into her pillow, closed her eyes, and struggled to place the vaguely familiar voice. "Uh ... good morning." This better not be a very jolly groom calling about a very stupid wedding detail that could easily be discussed at a more civilized hour of the day.

"This is Ned Wagner. I hope I'm not calling too early."

Ned Wagner. Vice president at the agency? Her heart began to pound. She sat bolt upright and tried to force her mind to function. Pulling the phone away from her head for a second, she cleared her throat as quietly as possible. "No. No. I've been up for a while."

"Super. Because I've got a proposition for you."

She scrambled to get a pencil and pad of paper from the nightstand drawer. "What's up?"

She'd never gotten a call at home from the VP before. Hell, she'd only rarely heard from him in the office, either. This was not a man who mingled in the trenches. His time was spent reeling in the big clients and then keeping them happy.

"Don't know if you've heard, but Avalon Cosmetics is having second thoughts about their new agency."

"I did hear something about that. Didn't know if it was true or not."

"It's true. So true, they want to come back."

"Cool!" *Cool?* Couldn't she think of something more professional to say than *cool?* How about, *That's wonderful news.* Or, *How exciting.* Or even, *That's thrilling.*

"We're all pretty excited about it," he said.

There was that *excited* word.

"Thrilled actually," he continued.

And the *thrilled* word. She studied a crack running the length of the ceiling.

"We've had a couple of meetings with them. Yesterday they asked us to be their agency of record again."

"They're coming back? That's *wonderful* news," she said in her most professional voice. Did it mean something for her? Why was he calling?

"They said we had the best group of people they'd ever worked with. And—"

Her heart was pounding so hard she could hear it in her ears. He couldn't possibly be about to say what she thought he was about to say.

"—they want their entire team back. We need you, Delaney. Are you available? Interested?"

She opened her mouth wide and punched the air with

her left hand. Interested? She was ready to do cartwheels. "I've taken another position, actually." She tried to keep from sounding totally and completely ecstatic.

"We want you back," Ned said. "And we'll raise your salary ten percent to make your decision easier."

Unbelievable. It was like she'd won the lottery!

"So are you in? Can we tell Avalon you'll be back?"

"Yes. Absolutely. Tell them I can't wait to get started." She threw off her covers and jumped out of bed to push aside the curtains. June sunshine and a warm breeze streamed through her open window. This was all she'd ever wanted.

"We're setting up an internal meeting with the whole team to get everyone up to speed. Can you be here Friday afternoon?"

Wait. "You mean in three days?" She paced the room, working schedules in her head. Okay, she could fly into Boston on Thursday night, attend the meeting Friday morning, then fly back here Friday afternoon in time for the rehearsal dinner. It would be a stretch, but doable.

With only two weddings left after this weekend, she'd be able to finish those out and then rejoin the agency in a couple of weeks. She could go back to Boston, back to her life, back to her job, back to a higher salary—and she'd have all that plus a hundred thousand dollars in the bank. "Friday should be fine. Just have to check my schedule, but I don't think I have anything so important I can't move it." *Liar, liar, pants on fire.*

"Good, we leave on Saturday for Tokyo."

'Tokyo?" Surely they weren't going to the Avalon

headquarters already. They didn't even have any advertising concepts to present yet.

"Sorry about the short notice. We're meeting at Avalon on Monday. It's actually more complicated than I've told you so far." Ned cleared his throat. "Their top management has concerns about marketing direction. They've got a new line of cosmetics they want to bring to market, and after firing the new agency so quickly, nerves are rattled. They've asked to have this initial meeting in their offices, hoping it'll settle everyone down."

"We get to roll out a new line?" This was like a dream come true.

"Yeah, everything. Package design, POS, digital, print, direct mail, TV, radio ... you name it, we'll be doing it."

Actually, it was more than a dream come true, it was a miracle. Delaney turned an awestruck circle in the middle of her room.

"That's why we want you back on Friday—we need to strategize before we go."

Reality crashed the party in her brain. She could force the Friday meeting into her schedule, but she couldn't be gone this weekend, not with a wedding to oversee. She dropped onto the edge of the bed and tried to still her racing heart. "Um, Tokyo may be a problem." Hearing her words out loud, she cringed. The client always came first.

"I know this is short notice. But they're the client. They say jump and we ask how high." Ned chuckled.

How well she knew that. Delaney put a hand to her forehead. This wasn't how things were supposed to happen.

"We need you there, Delaney. We need the account executive there so that everyone gives their blessing to this changeover," Ned said with sudden intensity. "It's not one hundred percent yet. Close, but not there. We can't risk anything going wrong."

How could she say no? How could she turn down the job she so desperately wanted and needed?

But how could she desert Mike and the others?

"Delaney?"

"Yes?" she answered, stalling.

"If there's something you need to finish up before you come back, we can get by without you on Friday. But you have to be on that plane with us Saturday."

Though she didn't respond immediately, she knew what her answer was going to be. "Right. I'll be there. Friday, Saturday, whenever you need me."

By early afternoon, she was a mess. She'd spent hours second-guessing her decision and trying to find some way to do everything, to make everyone happy, to keep the job at the agency and, somehow, still finish the weddings. She couldn't concentrate, could barely think, and the phone kept ringing with one wedding-related call after another.

Finally she grabbed her sunglasses, shoved some money in her pocket, and took off with no specific destination in mind. Swinging into the coffee shop, she grabbed an iced latte and headed to the park to work out the conflicts knotting her brain. As she passed the pond with its mother ducks and broods of ducklings, she envied the simplicity of their lives. Fly, swim, eat, lay eggs, raise babies.

Hide from hunters.

Okay, so maybe life wasn't easy for them, either.

She took in a deep breath of summer—clean air, blooming flowers, warm dirt, new-mown grass.

What should she do?

How could she tell Mike and the others she was leaving, and that because of her, none of them would get their inheritance?

How could she stay here when the job she desperately needed to get out of debt had just landed in her lap?

What if she didn't go to Tokyo and the agency lost its chance to regain the account because she hadn't come along?

What if she didn't go to Tokyo and the agency got the account back and offered the job to someone else?

What if she stayed for the wedding planning and the Henrys didn't finish their part and she didn't get her inheritance, anyway? And then she had no job and no money?

She squeezed her eyes shut.

What about whatever was going on between Mike and her?

Forget that. There was nothing going on between Mike and her.

Her brain felt like a spinning top.

She wandered across the park to where the old band shell had been demolished. A construction trailer was on-site, ready for the building phase, while a bulldozer loaded debris into a dump truck. She stopped to study a large sign showing an architectural rendition of the finished band shell.

"Pretty snazzy, huh?" a voice called. "The new one will be bigger than the old one, with much better sound."

She turned and smiled at Stonewall and Sully coming toward her from the construction trailer.

"Hey, guys. Looks like you're almost ready to start building."

Sully rocked back on his heels. "Just about."

"Finally." Stonewall tugged at one of his long white eyebrows. "It took forever to get the city workers out here to tear the old one down."

"It didn't take *that* long," Sully countered.

Delaney wanted to scream. She had no patience today for the bickering of these two.

"The old band shell was falling apart," Stonewall said. "Decayed wood, holes in the stage decking. It's been unsafe for years."

Delaney waited for Sully's counterargument.

"He's right about that," Sully said. "Problem was, the city just didn't have the money to build a new one."

Her mouth dropped open.

"Thank goodness for Ellie." Stonewall waved a hand at the construction site.

"Yes, where would we be without Ellie?"

Delaney knew she was gaping. They'd just had a breakthrough of sorts. She should tell Mike.

"So what brings you out here today?" Sully asked. "Want to check our progress? Hoping for a tour?"

"Of our demolished band shell?" Stonewall muttered.

She debated how to answer. "Just taking a walk. Need to figure some things out."

"Wedding stuff?" Stonewall pulled off his baseball cap and wiped his forehead with the side of his hand. "Hot out here today."

She shook her head. "Life stuff."

"We can help you with that," Sully said. "Done our share of living."

"Oh, that's okay. But thanks anyway."

"No, really. We have a method for making decisions," Stonewall said. "Henry Clark came up with it years ago."

Sully nodded.

These two were getting along way too well. "By any chance, does this decision-making method involve a bottle of Jameson?"

The two men exchanged a look. "How did you know?" Sully asked.

"Finest Irish whiskey there is." Delaney grinned.

Stonewall grinned back at her. "We just had some ourselves at lunch."

She never would have guessed. "Okay, so what's this method you guys are talking about? I'm a little desperate."

"Well, we call it the three-step doctor's method," Stonewall said.

"Was one of you a doctor?"

"No." Stonewall stuck his hands in the pockets of his baggy jeans. "But Henry Clark was smart enough to have been one."

"I see," she said, even though she didn't.

"It works like this." Sully held up his index finger. "Step one, you list the pros. Step two, you list the cons. Step three, you do no harm." He raised another finger with each new step.

"Do no harm?"

"If anything, either pro or con, will cause harm to someone else, that option is eliminated."

Delaney cocked her head, impressed. "First do no harm. the doctor's creed. How'd you guys come up with this?"

Sully let out a snort. "Stonewall had his heels dug in one night—"

"Now, just wait one minute," Stonewall said.

"Fine. He and I couldn't agree one night," Sully said.

"You two? I can't believe it."

"And Henry Clark, fine man that he was, pulled out the Jameson," Sully said with an Irish brogue. "And after a wee bit o' Jameson—"

"Many wee bits o' Jameson," Stonewall interjected.

"Many wee bits o' Jameson," Sully agreed, "we'd figured everything out."

"I guess I better get a bottle." Delaney examined the artist's rendition again. "So, you going to have this thing finished by the Fourth?"

"Without a doubt," Sully answered at the same moment Stonewall said, "When pigs fly."

Delaney laughed. "Thanks for your help, guys. I'd better get back to wedding planning and leave you to your work." She headed across the park thinking about the Henrys' decision-making process. It probably worked great for black-and-white issues.

"But what happens when every option has the potential to harm someone else?" she murmured aloud. "Then what do you do?"

20

THE REST OF THE DAY WENT BY IN A HAZE AS DELANEY agonized over whether she should call the ad agency and turn down the job. Pro-by-pro, con-by-con, she debated each side of the argument, finding each one strong in its own right. By eight o'clock when Mike picked her up to sneak onto the grounds of Harris House and put detection powder on the timer, she was still struggling with the decision.

Mike pulled into a parking space outside the mansion and shut off the engine. "I scoped it out already. Dan was right—the timer's on the outside wall of the carriage house, right next to the gas and electric meters."

Delaney studied the imposing stone building. "Are you sure we're not doing this too soon? It's only Tuesday. My uncle probably won't try to mess with it until Friday." *The day she was supposed to be back in Boston.*

Mike's eyes met hers. "I've got a game tomorrow night. Thursday and Friday night they have big functions here. Way too many people will be around. We'd never get away with it. It's got to be tonight."

Why was everything so urgent? Ever since she learned yesterday that the caterer had gotten shut down, her life had moved into a new level of out-of-control. She wished she could tell Mike what was going on, get his opinion about what to do. But she knew his answer would be completely subjective—stay and finish the weddings. And she couldn't blame him. If she were in his position, she would say exactly the same thing.

Mike pulled some green latex gloves from a paper bag on the floor. "SpyWizard said you have to be careful with the powder," he said.

"You'll practically be invisible out there with those neon signs on your hands," she said.

"The hardware store was out of clear ones, so I got these from my dentist."

"Always thinking. You probably left a real hole in the legal world when you quit that Chicago law firm."

He flashed a mock glare at her, and the sparkle in his eyes went straight to her heart.

"I just wish I'd listened to you earlier," he said. "We might have caught the guy already."

She wondered whether he'd still be impressed with her if he knew she was planning to leave in two days, leaving him and the other heirs high and dry. Guilt tweaked at her conscience.

He opened a bag and pulled a small plastic jar of gray powder and a long-bristled brush. "Okay, I'll go dust the timer. You keep a lookout."

"Maybe we should wait until dark. So we don't get caught and charged with defacing property or something."

"They close at nine and lock the gates. If we get caught

then, it'll be for trespassing *and* defacing property." He reached across the space between their seats and patted her leg. "Ready?"

"As I'll ever be."

They got out of the car and met at the front bumper.

"Just act like you're browsing the grounds." Mike jammed the gloves, jar, and brush in the back pocket of his jeans.

"Yeah, me and the guy with the green hands."

They followed a stone path weaving through the back gardens. Even this early in the season, the beds were spectacular, a stunning mix of colors and flowers.

Mike nodded his head to the left. "The carriage house is that way. If anyone looks like they're headed that direction, your mission is to stop them."

"No problem," she said with more confidence than she felt.

She wandered toward a flower garden designed around a white statue of a man in a toga. Tipping her head back, she pretended to study its lines. Out of the corner of her eye, she spotted a couple strolling arm-in-arm down the path toward her. She stepped in front of them to block their passage. Her mouth began to speak before her brain even knew what she was going to say. "I'm sorry, but the grounds are closing."

"I thought they were open until nine," the man said.

"Not on Tuesdays. Tuesdays it's eight-thirty." Delaney laughed nervously. "People always get it mixed up. That's why I'm out here ... so no one gets locked in for the night."

"Is the museum closing, too?" the woman asked.

Was it? She frantically considered her choices.

"Actually, it's open until nine, so feel free to look around inside."

They headed toward the building and Delaney exhaled in relief. Where was Mike? How long could it possibly take to brush a little powder on a timer?

Within minutes, a man in a dark business suit came striding down the path from the direction of the mansion. Adrenaline shot from one end of her body to the other. This didn't look positive.

"Excuse me," he said as he neared. "Are you the woman telling people the grounds close at eight-thirty?"

Delaney blanched. "You mean they don't?"

"No. Nine o'clock every night." His eyes narrowed and Delaney knew she had to get legitimate fast. Her thoughts tumbled over themselves.

"I'm so sorry. I'm new in town. I shouldn't have spoken without knowing for sure." She stuck out a hand. "Delaney McBride. I've, uh, taken over the Storybook Weddings shop from my late aunt, Ellie Clark. I'm checking out the grounds for ... photo backdrops for the wedding I'm overseeing this weekend."

As he shook her hand, his expression visibly eased. "Ohh. I'm the facilities manager. We're the site of a lot of wedding photography. If you want to call and make an appointment during the day, I can take some time to show you around. Point out some of the more popular photo areas."

"Thanks, I'll definitely do that. As long as you're open another half hour, I think I'll just wander around some more." As soon as the manager was out of sight, Delaney charged along the path toward the carriage house, almost running headfirst into Mike.

"Let's go," he said in a low voice, never breaking his stride. He pulled off the gloves and balled the green latex in his fist.

"Well?" she asked.

He didn't answer until they were driving away. Then he grinned. "Mission accomplished."

"Was the timer locked up?"

"Nope. Just opened the cover and there it was. Could have changed the times for every day of the week if I wanted to."

"Then what took so long?"

"The powder is messy. It was going everywhere. Then I dropped the container and it spilled in the grass and when I was trying to clean it up I tore my glove on a rusty screw." He held up the index finger of his right hand. "This should be purple in no time."

As a violet circle began to appear like magic on the tip of his finger, Delaney began to laugh. "What a pair we are. I was on the verge of being thrown off the grounds." She described her confrontation with the manager. "So now I have to make an appointment. Like I have time for another meeting what with the catering problems and other things I have to organize." *Like there was any point in her having a meeting if she was leaving town.*

"The new caterer will work out fine." Mike glanced at her and smiled. "By Saturday night, everything will be over, the bride will be happy, and this new pressure will be gone."

She nodded. Yeah. One way or another, this new pressure would be gone. The question was, would she?

———

Wednesday night, top of the ninth, score: six to four, two men on base, and two outs. Sitting next to Andie in the stands, Delaney leaned forward, elbows on her knees. "Your dad looks just like he did in high school right now," she said, grinning.

In his dark blue pin-striped jersey, cap pulled low on his forehead against the glare of the lights, Mike was confidently owning second base.

"He says he used to play better," Andie said.

"That double play was pretty impressive. I think they'll be celebrating at Ollie's tonight."

"Are you gonna go?" Andie looked at her sideways.

Delaney shrugged. She probably shouldn't—not knowing she was probably leaving on Friday.

"I think my dad wants you to go."

She smiled at Andie. If only she could figure out a way not to let Mike down—not to let everyone down. "I've got a few worries right now ..."

"Everything always works out for the best. That's what my dad says."

Yeah, but the problem was getting to the worked-out stage.

"This could be it, last out." Grinning, Andie raised a fist.

With the count at three balls, one strike, the batter took his time choosing his pitch. He swung hard and popped the ball up high and center. The center fielder positioned himself underneath and waited until the ball fell neatly into his glove, ending the game. As the crowd erupted in clapping and cheers, it dawned on Delaney that, for all the batter's efforts to find the perfect pitch, he'd still struck out.

Kind of felt like her life. The bases were loaded and she was trying to juggle balls and strikes and somehow bring everyone home. And inside she knew, just like the batter, she wasn't going to pull it off.

"Let's go find my dad."

Delaney followed Andie down the bleachers. It was time to accept reality. There was no way she could do both things.

Besides, she rationalized, it was unlikely that Millie would be able to successfully pull off the wedding dinner, even with Annalisa's help. Once this weekend's bride tasted her food, the odds were zero to none that Delaney would get a passing grade. Even if a miracle occurred and the bride didn't deliver the kiss of death, it was almost a given that the Henrys would. There wasn't enough Jameson in the world to keep them congenial long enough to finish the band shell by the Fourth of July.

Whatever her great-aunt had been trying to do with this will hadn't worked. Her entire estate would go to her brother, which was probably where it should have gone in the first place.

So. The decision was made. She would return to her job in Boston, go back to the life she loved—the high-powered advertising world. Her throat tightened.

Andie high-fived Mike. "Nice job," she said in a serious voice.

"Thanks coach." He pulled off Andie's baseball cap and used it to tap her playfully on the head.

"Yeah, great game," Delaney said. "You guys still have it."

"You coming down to Ollie's?"

She shook her head. *I think I'll go home and have a cry.* "Not tonight. I've got too much to do."

"I'll let you win at pool."

She felt a twinge under her breastbone and refused to be affected by it. No. She'd made this decision the smart way, without emotion, without giving any weight to the things that had happened between her and Mike. Because those things never lasted. She didn't want to look back later and realize she'd given up everything that mattered to her for a chance with Mike—a chance that never really existed in the first place.

21

Late the next morning, Mike was deep into writing a letter on behalf of a client when Delaney dropped by his office. In a breezy skirt, sleeveless top, and sandals, she was the picture of casual summer.

"Looking for the best in legal advice?" he asked with a grin.

Her lips curved up, but the smile didn't reach her eyes. "Do you have a few minutes to take a walk? There's something I want to talk to you about."

"Sure." He told his assistant he'd be back in half an hour, then followed Delaney outside.

After covering a block in silence, he decided to dive in. "So, what's up? Is there a new problem with the wedding?"

She avoided looking at him. "How's the car renovation coming along?"

"Going good. We'll be done in time for the parade."

As they walked down the sidewalk and he waited for Delaney to explain what was going on, he glanced into the stores they passed—gift shops, clothing stores, a pharmacy, a restaurant, the bank—all housed in sturdy, brick buildings built in the 1920s. This was a good town, a comfortable community, an uncomplicated way of life. He was glad he'd come back, for his own sake as well as Andie's.

For the first time in a long time, he remembered how his ex-wife had never liked coming here to visit. He'd been foolish enough then to think their love and a child would overcome any obstacles they faced.

"And the Henrys? How are they doing?" she asked.

"I'm not sure. The more I try to get a handle on it, the less I seem to learn. Stonewall claims they have it under control."

They stopped at a street corner and waited for a couple of cars to pass. Delaney turned to him. "But do they? I was out at the band shell Tuesday and construction hasn't even begun yet."

He winced.

"See, there's the thing," she said. "Even if you restore the car, and even if the new caterer is incredible and I manage to pull off a miracle, the Henrys aren't going to succeed."

"It's too soon to say that."

"Don't kid yourself. You know it, I know it. The only reason we can't say it's fact yet is because the deadline hasn't passed," she said, an edge in her voice.

"You don't know these guys—"

"I know enough. What they need is a five-star general type of project manager to oversee them every step of the way. Otherwise they're never going to get there."

"That's pretty judgmental." What was with her this afternoon? "Is something wrong?"

"No. It's just ... I can't wait around for those two to pull it together."

"What does that mean? You want to be their project manager *and* the wedding planner?"

She looked into his eyes, questioning. "No. Not me. I don't have time."

He shoved a hand through his hair and tried to figure out where the conversation was going.

"My job is important," she said out of the blue. "Not just to me, but to the company where I work."

"I thought you didn't have a job."

She looked ahead down street, Main Street, the place where he and Dan had to drive the restored Chevy in the Fourth of July parade. Suddenly he realized why she wanted to talk to him, knew the words she was going to say before they even left her mouth.

"I'm leaving," she said.

"Back to your job."

She nodded.

"Back to the fast lane." Disappointment slid through him. He should have known the corporate world was like the siren's call for her.

"The client that left the agency, the one I lost my job over ... it's coming back. They want the same team working for them. The agency needs me."

"There are people who need you here, too."

She turned away as if to block his words. "You don't understand. They want the agency to introduce a whole new product line. I need to make a living. There's no guarantee we'll get the inheritance if I stay. I have to go. I love my job."

Her tone was calm and matter-of-fact, as though they were discussing taking a vacation and not her leaving Birch Harbor forever. He looked at her, speechless, almost fascinated by how she had rationalized her decision—and disconnected herself from the impact that her departure would have on the rest of the heirs.

"I need to be in Boston to catch a flight Saturday afternoon to Tokyo, to meet with Avalon's executives."

"So you're leaving ... when?"

"This afternoon. It's an eighteen hour drive so I'm going to need two days."

"And the wedding Saturday? What happens there?" He shoved fisted hands into his pockets.

She shook her head. "I'm really sorry about the wedding, but I don't think my absence will matter. Lauren can handle everything—there's virtually nothing left to do. Sooner or later, something was bound to go wrong with one of the weddings that I couldn't fix and that would have been the end anyway. Besides, the Henrys will never be done in time."

So many excuses. "You won't even try?"

He glimpsed a glimmer of indecision in her expression before she glanced away. "It's not that simple. I need to be at this meeting to show Avalon management that changing agencies for the second time in six months won't result in more turmoil."

"And there's nothing more important than the job."

"Please tell me you understand."

"Do what you need to do, Delaney. And justify it any way you want. Just don't ask me to understand."

Her anger flared. "No, I suppose you wouldn't

understand someone wanting success in their chosen field. Not when you gave up your career to live in Birch Harbor."

"Is that what you're calling your decision? Success?" He snorted out a laugh. "You may know all about advertising, Delaney, but you have a lot to learn about success."

He walked away and didn't look back. How had he ever thought Delaney was anything other than a self-centered woman who only cared about what was in it for her? He'd been a fool to get involved.

———

What did Mike want from her? Delaney stood at the coffee shop counter and studied the menu on the wall without reading a word. She'd tried. She'd given it her all. Every time a roadblock appeared, she'd climbed over it as best she could. But no matter how hard she worked, the roadblocks kept coming.

"What can I get you?"

She jerked her attention to the clerk behind the counter. She needed caffeine so she could stay awake through the first leg of her drive to Boston. "A double latte, please."

She wanted this inheritance, wanted all of them to get their inheritance. She hated hurting Mike and the others, even the Henrys. But she really needed this job.

She had weighed everything and made a decision. A good, solid, fact-based decision. In the long run, this would be best for all of them. Better that they stop pretending *now* that they were going to get an inheritance. Because the Henrys' inability to work together and her uncle's—or someone's—determination to sabotage her success made counting on the inheritance way too much like taking your money and putting it all on red.

———

Mike stood in the kitchen doorway, hands in his pockets, and watched Andie writing a book report on the computer. He cleared his throat.

She twisted in her chair. "Daddio! How come you're home?"

Her personality had blossomed the past couple of weeks, and even homework was rarely an issue anymore. He knew it shouldn't be as simple as her working for Delaney, didn't *want* it to that simple. But it was.

"You think kids are the only people who ever get a half day of school?"

"You're done working?" Her eyes opened wide.

He laughed and shook his head. "No. Just kidding. Where's Grandma?" He was hoping his mom would agree to help Lauren oversee the wedding this weekend.

Andie saved her document and spun back to face him. "In the backyard. What happened?"

He shook his head and started to turn away. "Nothing."

"Dad, what's the matter?"

Shit, the kid could smell bad news a mile away. He sighed. He didn't want to tell her that Delaney was leaving town, was leaving them all without finishing the job. The last thing he wanted to do was tell the child he loved that another woman was stepping out of her life, that another woman she cared about had put her job first.

"Did Delaney call about me working tomorrow? We have a lot to finish for the next wedding."

He shook his head. "I have to talk to you about something," he said.

Andie's eyes grew round, as though she knew an important conversation was coming. "Delaney's nice." She jumped out of her chair to grab a bag of pretzel twists from the cupboard and shove a couple in her mouth. "And smart, too. I didn't have to work today. I hope she decides to stay here after all the weddings, don't you?"

He nodded slowly. He hadn't let himself think that far ahead, but, yeah, deep down he'd been hoping she would decide to stay. "Honey, I have some bad news. Delaney's leaving."

Andie froze with her hand in the bag. She looked up at him with innocent child's eyes. "How can she leave? There's still weddings to do."

"She got offered her old job back. The advertising agency where she used to work needs her."

"But what about the weddings? What about us?" The stricken expression on her face felt like a knife in his side. "We'll be okay. We'll get by without the inheritance. We didn't have it before, and there's no guarantee we would have gotten it, anyway."

"Not the inheritance, Dad." Andie's voice quavered. "What about *us*?"

He swallowed the lump lodged in his throat. "We," he said, "will be fine. She was just the lady who worked at Storybook Weddings for a while. But we've got each other. We're a team, you and me. We'll always have each other." He wrapped his daughter in his arms.

Andie nodded against his chest. He smoothed her hair and tried to tamp down his own anger, hurt, self-recriminations. He should never have let his daughter get so attached to Delaney.

"I thought she liked us," Andie whispered.

"She *does* like us. But her job is important to her. And people have to make decisions that are right for them." After a long minute he said, "Hey, you want to go out for pizza tonight?"

She shrugged against him.

"And then watch a movie?"

"What about my homework?" There was a touch of sarcasm in her voice. "And don't you have a stupid heirs' meeting later tonight?"

Oh, kid, he wanted to say, *screw your homework. Screw the meeting. Tonight we're going to tell the rest of the world to get lost. We're going to take some time, just the two of us, to focus on what's important. And it isn't jobs, it isn't inheritances, and it sure as hell isn't homework.*

"How much do you have?" he asked.

"Not that much."

He gave her ponytail a tug. "Okay, you keep working. I have to talk to Grandma, and then I have to run down to the station to talk to Dan, and then I do have to finish some work. But we're doing pizza tonight and then a movie, okay?"

"What about your meeting?"

"With this news, it'll be over quick."

She wiped the back of her hand across her eyes. "Did she leave because of you?"

"No. She got her old job back."

"It's because you—"

"No, honey. I don't think anyone could have made her stay."

"Love could have."

"Love? It's not that simple." *Not for women like Delaney.*

Andie pushed away from him, her shoulders hunched like a wall between them. "You're even dumber than I thought. I'm going to finish my homework."

22

MIKE CLIMBED INTO THE DRIVER'S SEAT OF THE CHEVY and was instantly catapulted back to the day he'd driven Delaney out to Sunset Point, the day he realized he'd been kidding himself that he was spending time with her just to make sure she'd stick around long enough to oversee all the weddings. He hadn't been able to stop thinking about her ever since.

And now she'd left town.

He started the engine.

Dan walked over and rested his hands on the frame of the open window. "What are you doing?"

"We would have had it restored in time. Ellie would have been so proud. Makes no difference anymore whether we drive it in the parade or not. But I thought, with Delaney leaving, I'd take one last spin before we have to turn it over to Joe Waverly. You want to go?"

"Sure, what the hell." Dan went to the passenger side of the car and got inside.

Five minutes later they were on the open highway, the top down and the radio blaring an oldies station.

"How's the new baby?" Mike asked.

"Slept four hours in a row last night."

"I remember those days. Thought I'd never get a full night's sleep again."

"Yeah, and now Andie's eleven."

"Going on twenty-nine," Mike said. "She blames me for Delaney leaving."

Dan nodded. "Smart kid, that one."

"I'm not responsible—she took a job."

"She's been nuts about you since she was eight."

"Childhood infatuations don't necessarily translate into adult relationships. Anyway, she wasn't worth the risk." Mike turned the radio down.

Dan snorted out a laugh. "The risk?"

"Andie and I have a nice, low key life. It's—"

"Boring." Dan turned his face into the wind coming over the side of the car.

"Calm, is what I was going to say. Delaney, on the other hand, is into climbing the corporate ladder and all the stress that comes with it."

"So given a choice, you'd go without love rather than take a risk. Doesn't sound like the Mike I used to know."

"That's not it."

"What is it, then?" Dan tapped his fingers on the armrest.

Mike gave his friend a sidelong glance. "My life is smooth ... secure."

"And predictable."

Predictable? "There's nothing wrong with predictable."

"Not a thing. Unless you like life dull. I just never thought it was your style."

Mike frowned. "Don't muddy the waters. Delaney is a whole other complication. Ever since her arrival, things have been upside down."

"And?" Dan pressed.

"And?"

"And maybe ... fun? When are you going to quit running away?"

Mike opened his mouth to make a quick comeback, but the words died on his tongue. His mind scrolled back to his divorce, to leaving Chicago, to coming home to Birch Harbor. Had he been running since his marriage ended?

"Delaney's not your ex," Dan said quietly.

He tried not to think about those days. The fighting, her coming and going with no regard for him or Andie, her job always first ... He never wanted to be with someone like that again.

No. That wasn't quite it. His mind wrapped around the thought and suddenly he realized the truth with such clarity that, for a moment, it felt like the car was no longer moving, like the wind was no longer blowing through the windows, like time was standing still.

The truth was, he hated what his life had become—and who he had become—when he was with her.

He sucked in a sharp breath.

"You okay?" Dan asked.

"Just figuring something out." It wasn't Delaney he was afraid of. It was himself.

"I repeat," Dan said, a knowing smile on his face, "you'd go without love rather than take a risk?"

Mike's grip tightened on the steering wheel. "Who said anything about love?"

Dan laughed.

"I'm not in love with Delaney," he protested.

"Keep telling yourself that. Maybe someday you'll begin to believe it."

Mike shook his head. "I may have been attracted to Delaney, but I can tell you this for sure—I am not in love with her."

Dan just laughed again.

———

Though she had her car packed by the afternoon, Delaney struggled to make herself leave. She hadn't told Andie she was going, hadn't even said goodbye to her. But after her conversation with Mike went so badly, she had no business showing up at his house—it would be overstepping of the greatest magnitude. She walked through the shop one last time, trying not to think about the disappointment her aunt would have felt upon learning Delaney had quit.

The shop phone rang and she quickly picked it up.

"Delaney, this is Annalisa. We have a little problem for Saturday."

She debated whether to cut the conversation short and just tell the woman she was going back to Boston. "What's wrong?"

"There's been a misunderstanding. When you said Millie wanted me to help with the food preparation ... I thought that meant she had taken over the entire job and her staff would be serving at the wedding. But she thought she was just cooking and that my staff would be serving—"

"No. Don't tell me—"

"We both told our servers they wouldn't be needed. Now we don't have enough help for the wedding. We've been asking everyone we know, but so far, we're not having much luck. That's why I'm calling."

Delaney blew out a breath. If it wasn't one thing with this job, it was another. "Annalisa, I'm really sorry, but I'm leaving town in a few minutes. Lauren Hobart will be handling everything from here on out. I'll leave a message for her about this, but you'll just have to do the best you can."

As soon as she hung up, Delaney let herself out of the shop and locked the door. Guilt and regret sat like nagging twin sisters on her shoulders; Lauren had a new baby for God's sake, she didn't need to be the point person for the rest of the weddings, too.

There just wasn't anyone else who could do it, and Delaney was up against a wall. If she didn't go to Boston now, she wouldn't get her job back. She forced herself to concentrate on the excitement of returning to the agency, on the upcoming meeting in Tokyo, on working with a client she truly liked ... and on leaving wedding planning and all its problems behind.

She gave the shop keys an angry shake. "And now what am I supposed to do with these?" she muttered. She didn't want to deliver them to Mike. She didn't want to give them to Lauren and Dan, either. Much as she believed in her decision, she wasn't ready to face any of them. That left her uncle. Though she didn't feel like facing him either, at least she wasn't likely to see disappointment in his eyes. He'd probably be overjoyed to learn she was pulling out.

She put a hand against the glass of the Storybook Weddings picture window and flashed back to the day she'd arrived, remembered how much she'd dreaded coming here, how she'd done it only for the inheritance. But now, even though she was on a path toward the future she'd always wanted, she was filled with conflicting emotions about leaving so soon. About disappointing so many people.

About never seeing Mike again.

As she approached her car, she spotted Andie racing toward her down the sidewalk. She pressed her lips together to hold back a rush of emotion. At least she would be able to say goodbye to the little girl whose company she had truly come to enjoy.

"My dad said you were leaving. Is it true?"

Delaney nodded.

"I wanted to say goodbye and ..." Andie stared at the ground and kicked a stone. When she raised her head, her eyes were wet with tears. "... and ask if you could stay."

Delaney swallowed hard. She opened her arms and took Andie in. "Sweetheart, thank you. I'm so glad you came. I wish I could stay, but I can't."

"Yes, you can." Andie's voice came out muffled against Delaney's shirt. She pushed back, her face scrunched with obstinacy. "You can stay if you want to. It's a choice you're making."

"Honey, it's my job. I need to make a living."

"It's your *choice*." Andie scrunched up her face and crossed her arms over her chest. "My dad says every time you choose to do something, you're also choosing not to do something else."

"Your dad's a wise man." Regret stabbed at her again.

"Why can't you choose to stay here instead? And choose not to go back there? Why can't you choose to make a living doing weddings?"

Delaney smiled at the naiveté of childhood. "I know it sounds easy to do that. But wedding planning isn't my background. The only thing I know about it is what I've learned the past three weeks. If my aunt hadn't set up everything in advance, if she hadn't been so organized, I never would have made it this far."

"I would help you."

"I know you would."

"I'm going to miss you. Really a lot." The quiver in Andie's voice betrayed the stoicism of her words.

"I'm going to miss you really a lot, too." Delaney pulled the girl into her arms again.

Andie sniffed and wiped her hand across her nose. She reached into the back pocket of her jean shorts, pulled out a crumpled piece of paper and handed it to Delaney. "This is my email address. Will you write me sometimes? Dad said I can get my own phone now that I'm eleven. If I send you my number, we could text."

"You bet. Whenever you want." She tucked the paper into her purse.

"I put down my address, too, just in case ..."

"Let me give you mine." Delaney pulled a grocery store receipt from her purse and scribbled her phone number and email address on it. "There," she said, handing it to Andie.

"Now we can stay in touch for sure. Come on, I'll drive you home."

As they stepped toward the car, Andie slid her hand into Delaney's. Tears pressed into Delaney's eyes; she blinked hard to hold them back, and gave the girl's hand a squeeze before reaching for the passenger door handle.

Andie shook her head. "I don't want a ride."

"You sure?"

Andie nodded, her tears beginning to fall. "See you, Delaney." She ran across the street, then yelled over her shoulder, "I love you!"

Delaney watched Andie run down the block and disappear out of sight around a corner. "I love you, too," she whispered.

That awesome kid deserved so much more than a text or e-mail or phone call every now and then. Delaney looked at the ground, at the keys in her hand, and drew a shaky breath.

She'd be better once she got out of town and even better once she got on the plane. She squeezed the shop keys in her hand until they dug in to her palm and headed for her uncle's office.

Taking the stairs two at a time, she charged through the door, intending to tell Uncle Joe she was leaving, deliver the keys, and get out. Claire looked up from her desk. Blue, the humping pug, charged straight for her.

Delaney stuck a foot out to fend off the dog until he gave up and trotted back down the hall. "Is my uncle around?" she asked.

"He's meeting with his financial adviser."

Well, wasn't this fortuitous? After he got all their

inheritances, he'd have plenty more to discuss with the guy.

Claire pointed at the clock on her desk. "They should be out soon. Joe has to be somewhere in half an hour. Can you wait?" She began to sort through some papers.

Delaney debated what to do. She wasn't looking forward to telling her uncle she was going back to Boston without finishing the weddings, dreaded seeing the look of triumph on his face when he realized he'd won. On the other hand, if she was wrong about him being the saboteur, she didn't want to leave town without saying goodbye.

"I'll wait a few minutes." She took a seat and picked up a magazine from the end table. Moments later, Blue was back wrapping his paws around her bare calf. Delaney tried to gently shake him off, but when that didn't work, she gave him a shove with her hand. "No!" she bit out in the lowest, sternest voice she could muster.

The dog cocked his head as though appraising her seriousness, then wandered over to Claire and plopped down beside her desk. Shit, she should have tried the alpha-male thing three weeks ago.

Joe's office door opened, and he and the financial advisor came into the room.

"Delaney! Hello!" Uncle Joe said as the other man went into the hall. "Is this a social visit or is there something I can do for you?"

Her uncle was either the best actor in the world or they were flat out wrong about him. She was glad she decided to say goodbye, just in case. She stood and put her purse over her shoulder. "I don't know if you heard ... Probably not, since I just told Mike a couple of hours ago."

She quickly explained what was going on.

"You're leaving?" Joe's forehead furrowed. "Without finishing?"

"Don't you have a wedding to do this weekend?" Claire asked in a high voice.

She nodded. "I tried to figure out a way to make everything work, but I can't. Lauren is taking over, I left notes for her about everything."

"But you'll lose your inheritance," Claire said.

"I don't have a choice. I've been out of work for more than three months. I need this job."

Her uncle's expression didn't change. "Ellie would have been disappointed. We'll be sorry to see you go. But, as a businessman, I understand."

Well. He sure wasn't making any effort to convince her to stay, was probably already popping open a bottle of champagne in his mind. Claire seemed more concerned about Delaney losing her inheritance than Uncle Joe did.

Delaney held out the keys. "I forgot to give Mike the keys to the shop and apartment. Can I leave them with you?"

Joe took the offered keyring and it disappeared into his large hand. He reached out to give her a hug. "I'll really sorry you can't stay," he said. "Keep in touch, Delaney."

Yeah, right.

Claire came out from behind the desk to give Delaney a hug, too. "Best of luck to you. Let us know how you're doing."

When she got back to her car, she felt a surge of overwhelming relief. It was over. This town held nothing for her anymore. No hopes, no dreams, no future. She headed for the highway, passing familiar landmarks along the way—the grade school, the old ice-cream parlor, the gas station on the corner, the fire station, the road to the old cemetery where they used to ride their bikes, the city-limits sign freshly painted in blue and gray: *Thank you for visiting Birch Harbor.*

"Thanks for having me," she murmured.

The last time she'd noticed that sign, she and her mother were moving out of town. As they passed the sign, she'd sobbed, and her mother had rubbed her shoulder and said, "Before long, you'll forget all about Birch Harbor and feel the same way about the next place we live." In that moment, Delaney had vowed she would never love any place again because it hurt too much when you left.

Thank you for visiting. In how many different cities and towns had she seen those words when she was leaving? In how many hotels and restaurants? In how many relationships—friends, lovers, coworkers—had it been implied?

Too many.

She punched the radio button and music flooded the car, burying her pain beneath its bouncing rhythm. Anything to keep her thoughts occupied so she didn't have room in her brain to think. An hour passed and then another, miles rolling away beneath her tires.

Thank you for visiting. The phrase crept into her brain in the way that dust blown off a newly plowed field seeps beneath closed windows.

She hadn't held true to her vow to never love again. She had loved more than one man, more than one city, but each time always less than the last.

She'd always been just a visitor.

23

———

Tears blinded her, and she pulled the car to the side of the road and put on the flashers. When had it happened? When had she become a visitor instead of a permanent resident? She searched her mind, but couldn't find any definitive moment. Just a series of decisions—choices, Andie called them—that kept taking her away from belonging anywhere or with anyone. Choices to not get involved, to not care. Choices that were, on the flip side, decisions to stay separate, unattached, alone.

From the moment she'd learned about Aunt Ellie's will, she hadn't wanted to take it on. Long ago she'd learned not to count on anyone but herself; it just made life easier. The will put her in an odd place—relying on others for her inheritance and, ultimately, happiness. And all those other people relying on her.

It had scared her. What did you owe people who relied on you? And, if they came through for you, what did you owe them in return? Your life? Happiness?

And what if you couldn't deliver? Or what if something went wrong?

Look at her cousin Nora. She'd fallen head over heels for a guy, embraced the whole married life thing—family, friends, and kids—and then he died, leaving her alone again.

Would Nora have chosen the same path if she'd known the outcome in advance?

Delaney sighed. Yeah, she would have.

She closed her eyes and let the tears fall. She'd spent the past fifteen years making sure she didn't make the same mistakes as her mother.

But was her life really any different? Or any better? She didn't belong anywhere—or with anyone. Had no close friends except her coworkers, and even they were more associates than friends. She had a job in Boston—but no real loyalty to the city.

Flashing red and blue lights reflected in the rearview mirror and she looked over her shoulder to see a sheriff's department squad car on the shoulder behind her. *Oh, just great.*

She reached for the door handle, intending to jump out and tell him nothing was wrong, but stopped herself at the last second. She'd heard cops didn't like it when people did that—made them nervous, like you might have a gun or something. She dragged a hand across her eyes to wipe away all trace of her tears, then smiled at the burly officer through the open window.

"Everything okay here?" he asked.

She nodded. "Yes. Just—just not sure which way I want to go."

"Where you headed? I can give you directions."

If only it were that simple. Her shoulders drooped. "You probably can't help me. I'm headed for Boston. But I'm not so sure where I'm going."

The deputy's face stayed expressionless. "That's a long way to travel without knowing where you're going. Maybe you oughta plug it into your phone's GPS. Or stop at the next town and get yourself a map. Plot your course, figure out where you want to stop and rest along the way."

"Thanks." She forced a smile.

"You'll get where you're going with a lot less hassle. Maybe even enjoy the trip. Good luck."

Delaney watched him in the side mirror as he returned to the squad car. "Thanks, but I have a map already," she murmured. And that's what seemed to be the problem. She'd left no space for detours, sightseeing, or adventures along the way. No room to discover if there was something out there other than what she'd already chosen. No time to find out if what she'd chosen was what she really wanted.

She hit the butt of her hand against the steering wheel. And what difference did it make knowing that about herself? She still needed to make money. And she had an incredible job offer waiting in Boston that would turn her life around.

She could stop being a visitor there.

She could stay with that job for a long time. Could make an effort to get to know her co-workers better. Could volunteer somewhere, and make friends outside work.

Except she was leaving her fellow heirs high and dry.

She slumped into her seat. She could be totally determined to end her *visiting lifestyle* in Boston, but she wanted to leave Birch Harbor full of friends. She wanted to help the others get their inheritances. She wanted to see the expressions on their faces when they knew they'd all succeeded.

What was she thinking? She couldn't go back to Birch Harbor. If she stayed to finish the weddings, she would have to give up the job. She'd have to keep flying trapeze without a net. And she'd still have all the other problems with the catering staff, the Henrys and someone trying to sabotage the weddings.

She let the Henrys' decision-making method roll through her mind. Pros and cons. If both options had the potential to cause harm, then the best choice had to be the one that caused the least amount of damage. The ad agency would probably get the account back whether she was there or not. But there was no way the heirs would get their inheritances if she left.

Maybe the agency would understand if she called and explained the situation. Maybe they would hold the job a few weeks if she told them what was at stake—not just for her, but for the others. And if not, well ...

She nodded to herself. She'd made a commitment to do the weddings. She owed it to her fellow heirs. *Her friends*.

It was the right thing to do.

So now what?

"Take charge, Delaney," she said softly. "Take charge." She pulled onto the road and drove a few more miles, and then suddenly, before she even knew she'd made a decision, she'd done a U-turn. She looked at her hands on the steering wheel and grinned. "Nice job, guys."

Her smile faded. What the hell was wrong with her

fingers? She turned her right hand palm up and examined it. Every finger was partially stained purple.

How did she get ink all over her hand? She pulled onto the shoulder again, dug a wet wipe out of the glove compartment and tried to clean off her fingers. The purple got darker. She frowned. If she didn't know better ...

Mike's words came back to her: *It only turns purple when it mixes with skin oils.*

She dropped the wet wipe on the floor. If she didn't know better, she'd think she had gotten into the detection powder. But when they did the job, they'd been in Mike's car, not hers. So how had she gotten this all over her—

Calf? A purple stain had appeared on her lower leg. Her heart started to hammer.

The dog. Her uncle. *The dog.* Omigod. Mike had spilled detection powder in the grass.

Oh. My. God. She had to tell Mike.

She looked at her purple fingers again. Oh, no, she didn't, she couldn't have— She flipped down the visor to look at her reflection in the vanity mirror; a violet stripe meandered across her eyelids. "Ohhh, beautiful. That's what I get for crying."

She wouldn't have to worry about telling Mike anything. He'd see it himself.

Shoving the gearshift into *Drive*, she jammed her foot down on the accelerator, eager to get back. With a couple of hours to think before she reached Birch Harbor, she turned her focus to the upcoming wedding. They still needed servers. She could wait tables if it would help. Mike and Dan could serve. And the Henrys—there were two of them.

That made five right there. Maybe forcing the Henrys to work together in public would help them get along better.

She could dream anyway.

Good thing it was only Thursday; she still had plenty of time to figure out a plan and pull it all together once she got back to the shop. She considered calling the agency to tell them of her change in plans, but decided to wait until she wasn't driving; she'd rather have pen and paper in front of her when she made the call, just in case they actually agreed and she needed to take some notes.

Passing the *Welcome to Birch Harbor* sign, she waved and said, "Damn glad to be here!" Then she drove past her uncle's office and held herself back from hanging out the window and shouting, *You can't get rid of Delaney McBride that easily!* They were probably gone already anyway.

And hell, they had her keys.

She parked in front of Storybook Weddings and called Annalisa. As soon as the woman answered, Delaney launched into her plan.

"But what if they don't agree to be servers?" Annalisa asked. "I'm a wreck over this."

"Leave it to me. Don't worry about it. You just get ready to cook. I'll talk to everyone and call you back the minute I have the serving staff finalized." She ended the call and grinned. This was getting fun.

She wiggled her purple fingers. And the fun wouldn't be ending anytime soon. Because next she was going to tell Mike about her uncle. She was going to tell him she was back to finish the weddings. And she was going to tell Andie, too. If she was lucky, she'd find them both at home right now.

Ten minutes later she was standing on Mike's front porch in the falling dusk, hands on her hips in frustration. The house was dark and no one answered the doorbell. They weren't at the service station, either—she'd driven past it on the way here and it was already closed for the night. Here she was with the best news ever and no one to share it with. She let out a sigh. They could be anywhere right now. She supposed she could call Mike's cell phone, but she'd much rather say everything in person. She glanced at her watch; it was just past seven.

Ohh, of course. *The heirs' meeting.* Mike was in the library meeting with the other heirs.

Exactly where she was supposed to be, too.

He probably already told them she'd skipped town. They were probably talking about it right now, hating her at this very minute.

And rightfully so.

This was *really* getting to be fun.

———

Mike waited patiently for the dull roar to subside.

"What do you mean, she quit?" Sully asked. "Get her back."

"Can't. She left town already."

"She told you and then took off? All in the same day?" Stonewall slouched down into his chair, disgusted. "I knew this thing was never going to work."

"We saw her Tuesday and she said she had to figure some things out. I thought it had to do with weddings," Sully said.

"Guess she figured them out." Mike restrained the anger that welled up inside him every time he devoted more than five seconds to thinking about Delaney quitting.

"Didn't she care about what this meant for everyone else?" Sully asked.

"To be honest, Sully, I think she figured you two were the ones who didn't care what happened."

"Us?"

Mike exchanged a look with Dan. "You were always bickering so much, she figured you'd never get the band shell built in time."

"I cared," Sully said.

"Me, too." Stonewall nodded. "We've always disagreed—"

"Yeah, but it didn't mean we weren't friends."

"Right."

"Guys, it's a little late for a lovefest," Dan said. "With Delaney gone, you can keep fighting till the day you die and it won't matter."

"So now you boys won't get the car or the money." Sully shook his head.

"We'll be okay. It's not like we already had it and have to give it back. Now that would be bad," Mike said.

"I can't believe she didn't need a hundred grand." Stonewall pulled absently at one of his eyebrows. "That's a lot of money to walk away from."

"I think she felt ... backed into a corner. She had to make a choice." Mike crossed the room. "Things kept going wrong with wedding planning. Then when the caterer got shut down, she figured the handwriting was on the wall."

"Didn't seem like the quitting type," Sully said. "She seemed like a fighter to me."

Mike shrugged. "Appearances," he said slowly, "can sometimes be deceiving."

———

Delaney reached the library and raced up the stairs to the second floor, drawing up short at the sight of the brown-haired girl bent over a book at a wooden table just outside the meeting room. She swallowed hard. "Hey, Andie," she whispered.

The girl raised her head, and her eyes rounded. She started to stand, then stopped herself. "Did you forget something? What's that on your eyes?"

"I didn't forget anything. I came back to do the weddings. And that purple stuff? I'll tell you all about it later." She bent to kiss the top of Andie's head.

Andie clapped her hands together. "Wait till my dad hears this. He's been pretty crabby all night."

"He has? Then I'd better get in there and change his mood, don't you think?"

24

———

THE DOOR BURST OPEN AND BANGED AGAINST THE opposite wall. Every head spun round to see what was going on. Delaney stood in the doorway like a conquering hero. *Hell, like Xena, the warrior princess,* Mike thought. The only thing missing was the skimpy outfit. Although the purple stripe across her eyes was a nice touch. And the shade seemed familiar ... He inspected the stain on the tip of his right index finger.

Same color.

What had Delaney been up to the past couple of hours?

"Seems like a fighter to me, too," Stonewall muttered.

Delaney strode toward the table, then fixed her gaze on each of the men in turn. "Gentlemen."

Andie leaned in the door to give Mike thumbs-up. He grinned back at her.

No one so much as breathed. Even the air in the room seemed to hang utterly still in anticipation. Andie sneaked inside and sat in the corner by the whiteboard to watch.

Delaney scowled at the Henrys, and the two actually

had the good sense to look afraid. As angry as he was with her for what she'd pulled earlier today, Mike felt a grudging admiration for the entrance she'd just made and the effect she was having on the men.

"I have a wedding to do this weekend." Delaney leaned forward to rest her hands on the table. "You've probably heard about the caterer being shut down. That's old news. I'm already onto a new crisis and I'm going to need everyone's help." She straightened.

"Anything you want," Stonewall said.

"We're here for you," Sully added.

She hesitated, caught off balance by their remarks. But she quickly recovered. "We have a shortage of servers for the wedding dinner. I need everyone to wait tables if we're going to pull this thing off and get a satisfactory rating." She pointed at each of the men in turn. "That means *everyone*."

"Yeah. Sure. Absolutely. No problem." The words tumbled out of them, one on top of the other.

Delaney's expression softened. A smile broke across her face, and she let out a quiet laugh. Mike didn't know what had brought her back, but he was glad she'd come.

Delaney raised her arms as though drawing everyone into a big hug. "All of you. Thank you. You're wonderful."

"No. Thank *you*," Sully said. "You're the one who's wonderful. We've been … well, less than that."

"I'm not so sure about that." Delaney's voice caught. "I know vinegar way too well and have a lot to learn about honey."

"Honey can be overrated," Stonewall said. "Sometimes what's needed is a dose of vinegar to clean off the mineral deposits and get the mechanism moving again."

"And who would know that better than you?" Sully muttered, standing.

Delaney laughed. "I promised to call the caterer the minute you guys agreed. So, if you'll excuse me ..." She went into the hall.

"Meeting adjourned," Sully said as the door closed behind her. He gave Mike a shove in the back. "This time, don't let her get away."

Mike chased Delaney out the door, almost crashing into her in the hall when she stopped to make a phone call. Spotting him, her face registered surprise.

"Hi," he said, taking a step back. "I thought you were leaving."

"Just calling the caterer. Hold on a sec." She finished leaving a message, shut off her phone and grinned at him. "Hey, didn't you tell me you have an extra set of keys to the wedding shop and apartment?"

"Yeah, at my house."

"I need to get those. I gave mine to my uncle."

"Why'd you do that?" he asked, when what he really wanted to say was, *You're incredible.*

"Stupidity. Sheer stupidity."

No, you're the most intelligent woman I know. "So, uh, what's with the stripe across your eyes?" He made swiping motion in the air.

"I'll give you one guess. It's not mascara." Delaney showed him her hands.

"Weren't you listening when I told you how easily that stuff spreads? So where'd you get it? Did you go back to the Harris House?"

She rolled her eyes. "I'll tell you when the meeting's

over."

"It's over. We've adjourned."

"Let's go outside. This is a story you're going to love."

They went down the stairs side by side, Andie tagging along behind.

"Thanks for coming back," Mike said. "I'm really glad you're here."

"Me, too." She smiled.

"Me three," Andie shouted.

"What about your job?" Mike looked directly at her.

"Yeah, I've got to call them tomorrow."

"They don't know you're not coming?" Andie slung her backpack over her shoulders.

"Not yet."

"Will they be mad?" the girl asked.

"Probably. They were depending on me. But people here were depending on me, too. And you know what?" She turned and tousled Andie's hair. "I care a lot more about the people here than the ones there."

Mike wanted to put his arms around her, to kiss her mouth, her cheeks, her hair. To pull her tight to him and run his hands down her back, under her tee-shirt. Instead he settled for putting an arm around her shoulders. "Delaney McBride, I think you've mastered the honey/vinegar ratio thing."

She grinned and pushed through the door outside. "Check out my right calf."

He'd already checked out both her legs weeks ago, but okay, if she insisted, he'd force himself to do it again. The same purple stain was on her lower leg. "You're covered with the stuff."

"Why do you have purple all over you?" Andie asked.

"I dropped my keys off at my uncle's office, remember?"

"Yeah. And?" Mike said.

"The dog."

Mike cocked his head. "The dog? What?" As he looked at the stain on Delaney's calf again, all the dots connected. "*I spilled the powder in the grass.*"

Delaney nodded knowingly. "The dog."

"Damn." Mike punched a triumphant fist in the air. "Well, if it's on the dog, it's on Joe's fingers. We've got that son of a bitch. Want to pay a visit in the morning?"

Delaney unlocked her BMW. "I'm right there with you. I'll follow you home to get the keys. Then, I'm going to unpack so we can hit the ground running tomorrow."

"Why does Delaney have purple all over her?" Andie fell into step beside Mike as they headed to their car.

"It's a long story," he said. "Come on, we've got a movie to watch."

God, he was glad Delaney was back. He hadn't fully appreciated how much he would miss her until she'd returned. Now he didn't ever want to let her go again. That's when it hit him; Dan had been right. Somehow, in the past three weeks, he'd fallen in love with Pumpkin McBride.

"The purple on your face is lighter this morning." Mike stopped on the sidewalk outside Joe Waverly's building and peered under Delaney's baseball cap.

"Thank God. Maybe because it's a third-hand stain.

From the dog, to my fingers, to my face." Delaney tugged the cap lower on her forehead. "What if we're wrong about my uncle? What if he just took the dog for a walk?"

"At the Harris House? A museum that doesn't allow pets on the grounds? Unlikely. Still, that's why we're not going to accuse him outright. We're just getting the keys back for you ... and engaging in some small talk."

"Right." Delaney fiddled with the brim of her cap again. "If my uncle's guilty, I want to catch him. But I hope we find out he isn't. I'm glad Aunt Ellie's not here to see this. It would devastate her."

"Don't cross too many bridges too soon." Mike locked his fingers around hers. "Come on, let's go in."

As they entered Joe's office space, Claire looked up in surprise, hands frozen at the computer keyboard. "Delaney? I thought you left town."

"I only got a couple of hours away before I changed my mind," she said.

"Is that Delaney I hear?" Uncle Joe stepped into the reception area, Blue dancing around his feet. He grinned and brought his hands together with a clap. "What brings you back?"

She tried to read his reaction. Happy and delighted? Or surprised and suspicious? Joe stuffed his hands into his pockets, and Delaney's stomach dropped. *Oh, Uncle Joe.*

"She changed her mind," Mike said just as she replied, "I didn't like running out on my obligations."

Blue zeroed in on Mike and began to jump excitedly at his legs. Delaney swallowed a laugh. Better him than her.

"That's good. Very good," Joe said.

"We just stopped to pick up the keys so she can get back

into the shop." Mike pushed the dog away with his foot.

"Blue! Bed!" Joe barked. The pug slunk away down the hall.

Joe got the keys from his office. A frown furrowed his brow and he bent to look under the rim of Delaney's cap. "You've got purple across your eyes."

"Yeah, I know."

"It's the same stuff I have all over my fingers." Joe held up his hands. "What is it? I thought maybe it was from changing the cartridge in the printer. But when I tried to wash it off, it just spread."

"It's called detection powder," Mike said slowly. "From the timer for the outdoor sprinkler system at Harris House."

"What are you talking about?" Joe asked. "I haven't been at Harris House in months."

Silence hung over them.

Delaney blew out a breath. "We think ... someone's been trying to sabotage the weddings," she explained. "And we were afraid they might set the sprinkler to go off during Saturday's event. So we put detection powder on the timer."

"It's invisible until it mixes with the skin's natural oil, then it turns purple. Pretty much nothing will remove it," Mike added.

He sounded so proud of himself, Delaney half expected him to pull out a decoder ring and spy club membership card. She would have laughed if only this weren't such a depressing moment.

"Honestly, I haven't been anywhere near Harris House, let alone the timer for their sprinkler system. I don't even know where that is." Joe frowned. "So how did it get all over me?"

"The same way it got all over me," Delaney said. "Your dog. Mike spilled the powder on the ground by the timer. That has to be where Blue got into it. I touched your dog yesterday and now my hands are stained. Look what happened where he was getting friendly with my calf." Delaney stuck out her leg.

"You think I'm trying to ruin the weddings? To make sure you don't succeed?" There was such sadness in his voice, Delaney wished she and Mike were wrong.

"You get the entire inheritance if the heirs fail." She couldn't bring herself to say, *You're the only one with motive.*

"No, I don't. There's more to this will than you realize. Only Ellie, her attorney, and I know the extent of it."

"More?" Mike, Delaney and Claire said together.

Exactly how much more could her aunt have come up with? Hadn't she already made life difficult enough?

"Ellie had a codicil written up."

"She made changes to the will?" Mike asked.

Joe rubbed a hand across his forehead. "She asked me not to reveal it until your deadline had passed."

"July Fourth," Claire said with a nod.

"I guess I should start at the beginning," Joe said. "Ellie wanted to leave a legacy of the love she and Henry shared. Of the friendships they had with special people in this town." He crossed the reception area and turned to face them. "We talked about a lot of ways for her to leave that legacy. It started with the car. She wanted the Chevy restored because it was the car Henry courted her in. That's what made her think of assigning duties to each heir."

"But how did I get in there?" Delaney asked. "I didn't

live in town. I didn't have much contact with her the last few years."

"When Mike moved back after his divorce, Ellie decided what he needed was to love again, to find the kind of relationship she and Henry had."

"She actually talked to me about that," Mike said.

"She remembered you once had feelings for Mike. And she realized during your visits here that you didn't have a lot of faith in the longevity of love." Joe smiled sheepishly. "So she set up her will to throw you and Mike together and hoped sparks would fly. Really none of her business, but what are you going to do with a romantic old woman?" His lips curved downward. "As for the Henrys, you've probably figured this out already. She wanted them to learn to get along without Henry Clark to mediate."

"Dan and I suspected as much," Mike said.

Joe put his hands in his pockets. "She had fun putting it all together. But she didn't want anyone to actually lose out if they couldn't accomplish what she'd asked."

Claire frowned. "But the will says—"

"That's the will. The codicil the attorney drew up, the one that I have, gives all heirs their inheritances whether they meet the terms of the will or not."

Delaney gasped.

"Damn," Mike said.

"You mean the weddings don't ... the band shell ... the '57 Chevy ... we all get ..." Delaney couldn't formulate a coherent thought.

"No. Yes. Whatever the question. The bottom line is, she loved all of you very much. She wanted you to finish the weddings, hoped you would fall in love with Mike—and with planning weddings. She really hoped you'd want to stay here. But in the end, she had no intention of withholding anyone's inheritance. No matter what happened, she wanted to make sure you had something to remember her by."

He looked from Delaney to Mike. "She loved you all too much to pull the rug out from under you like that."

"Oh, Uncle Joe, I'm so sorry. I just—I'm sorry," Delaney said.

"But then, why is there detection powder all over Blue?" Mike asked.

Hearing his name, the pug stole back into the room, wagging his tail low to the ground as if he knew he was in trouble.

Joe turned to Claire. "Do you have any idea how—?"

"It's possible," she said in a small voice, her eyes filling with tears, "that while someone was taking Blue for exercise yesterday, that person may have considered changing the timer." Her voice quavered. "That person may have stood there for a long time thinking about what to do. And then decided it was wrong and didn't do anything at all."

Nobody moved a muscle.

Claire held out her hands, not a speck of purple on them. "I didn't touch the timer."

"But why were you even thinking about doing it?" Joe asked.

"For you. So you could get the inheritance that should have been yours. So you don't have to go bankrupt."

"I'm not going bankrupt."

"You're not?" Claire looked confused.

"You almost ruined a wedding because you thought I

was going bankrupt?"

'Two weddings," Delaney said quietly. "Almost ruined two."

Joe jerked as though he'd been hit. "What do you mean?"

"The thermostat in the florist's cooler was turned down so low all the flowers froze before the wedding last weekend. And the wedding cake got canceled." She kept her eyes on her uncle. "And then, a few days ago someone anonymously reported the caterer for this Saturday's wedding to the Department of Health and got her shut down for having an unlicensed facility."

Joe turned stiffly to Claire. "Did you do all this?"

"I thought you were in trouble, that you needed money." Claire's voice shook and tears spilled over her cheeks. "When the soloist for the first wedding got laryngitis, it made me think. What if Delaney didn't get a passing grade from one of the brides? Then Ellie's money would go to you and your problems would be over."

"But, Claire, I own lots of property, office buildings. You know that. What made you think I was in trouble?"

"You're so worried about the market, always fussing with your accounts. We've been dating for eleven years, three months and four days. And you always say you don't want to get married until things are better. What was I supposed to think?" She pulled a tissue from her top drawer and blew her nose. "I wanted to help you. But when I walked Blue yesterday over to Harris House, I realized I couldn't live with myself if I ruined someone's wedding day. I decided you would just have to go bankrupt. I swear, didn't touch the timer."

Delaney gaped at Claire, incredulous.

Joe let loose with a huge belly laugh. "I fuss about my accounts because I like playing the market. And when I say I want things to be better, I'm talking about me. I need to feel right about marrying a woman so much younger than I am. I've been alone a long time. Pretty set in my ways."

"I don't care about any of that," Claire said.

Joe put an arm around her shoulder. "What you did was stupid and selfish and expensive. Either I make restitution or you go to jail. I should be furious with you. And a big part of me is."

"I'm sorry," Claire whispered. "I can't even believe I did some of that stuff."

Unspoken recriminations filled the silence.

"*Forgive quickly,*" Mike said in a soft voice. "*Kiss slowly ...*"

"*Love truly, laugh uncontrollably ...*" Delaney said.

An incredulous expression crossed Mike's face. "You know James Dean."

Joe looked from Mike to Delaney and back again. "*And never regret anything that made you smile.* Excellent advice for us all, I'm beginning to think." He reached a hand out to Claire. "I've been taking care of myself so long, I never realized you might worry. Honey, when you have questions, all you have to do is ask." He took her other hand. "If I marry you, will you stop getting such ideas?"

Her eyes widened and she nodded.

"Okay. Let me check my financial situation and I'll get back to you."

Laughter exploded across the room.

25

———

"Wait until Dan and Lauren find out about the codicil," Mike said.

"I still can't believe it." Delaney unlocked the door to the wedding shop. "We get our inheritance no matter what? I wish my aunt were here so I could hug her."

"Or yell at her. I'm not sure which."

Delaney nodded. "If we'd only known, I wouldn't ever have had to come back. I could have had the job of my dreams and the money from Aunt Ellie. Kind of like winning the lottery."

Mike chuckled. He felt like he'd won the lottery, too, but for him, it happened the moment Delaney arrived at the heirs' meeting last night.

He wanted to tell her how he felt, but there would be time later. For now, he'd just be happy she decided come back, that her job in the fast life didn't have the hold on her he'd thought it did. "To think I wouldn't have had to live and die over the Henrys and weddings for the past few weeks," he said.

"And I wouldn't have had to deal with those half-crazed perfectionist brides and their mothers." Delaney let out a delighted laugh. "Although, in retrospect, it was sort of fun."

"Am I hearing this right? Delaney McBride is admitting to enjoying wedding planning?" He slid onto one of the stools at the worktable in the back room. "So, what did the agency say when you told them you weren't taking the job?"

For a moment her face was blank. Then her jaw dropped in amazement. "I forgot to call. I got up this morning so focused on catching my uncle, I forgot all about it. *They still think I'm coming.*"

"Better let them know so they can make other plans."

"Mike! Now they don't need to!" She looked upward as though thanking the heavens. "My forgetting to call is a godsend. I can fly out to Boston today and still make the Tokyo flight tomorrow. I'll just leave my car at the airport. It doesn't matter *who* finishes out the weddings. I don't have to give up my job. I can still be the account exec for Avalon." She sat on the stool next to him and began to run a flight search on her phone.

Mike rubbed a hand across his eyes. He'd thought Delaney's decision to finish the weddings meant she'd made decisions about her life, where she was going, what was important. Thought she'd begun to see Birch Harbor—and maybe him—as things worth keeping.

"Why don't you stay?" he asked.

"What?" She lifted her head to look at him.

"Why don't you stay here?"

"In Birch Harbor? And do weddings? You know I thought about that yesterday and ..." She crinkled her nose and shook her head. "It's been fun ... sometimes. But I think

I just got my second chance. Karma or something. Fate telling me I was missing out on what my future was supposed to be and, here, take another shot at it."

"Your aunt worked hard to throw us together. Maybe that's karma, too."

She tilted her head. "I didn't think we were more than a passing moment. You had your life here. I had my life there. I didn't expect more because, well, I have aspirations. I know you have aspirations, too, but they aren't ... I'm sorry, I don't mean that the way it sounds."

If he wanted to, he supposed he could feel offended by her words. Instead, all he felt was disappointment. Fancy titles and lots of money no longer impressed him. What he appreciated now was a comfortable living, a stable home for his daughter, an unrushed lifestyle. He'd found that here. The only thing that would make it better would be a woman to share it with. *Delaney.*

But she wanted something else entirely.

"Don't worry about it," he said. "I'm sure plenty of people think that because I left a big law firm, I ran away from success. I don't care. I'm a lot happier now than I was then."

"That's good."

"I think you could be happy here, too. So stay. You've done a great job with the planning. You've got the Henrys working together. And ..."

"And?" She tilted her head.

"I know Andie wishes you would. And Dan and Lauren." He paused. "And I do, too. I wish you would stay."

She stared at him a minute, started to raise her hands in

a gesture of supplication before letting them fall to her sides. "I could visit."

Visit. He nodded slowly. Delaney was still chasing bigger, better, more. It was time to move on. "Visiting is always nice." He leaned over to kiss her lightly on the mouth. "Just remember, there's more to life than just making a living. Good luck in Tokyo, Delaney McBride. I'm going to miss you." *More than she would ever know.*

———

Delaney watched him leave, watched him turn down the street in the direction of Dan's service station. She sat at the work table, unmoving, as confusion crowded her mind, and she tried to sort out what had just happened and what she really wanted. She'd been given a second chance to make her mark in advertising. Opportunities like this were rare— and second chances even more so.

She could visit Mike anytime she wanted.

Visit. The way she had with every relationship, every job, every town in her life. She'd gone down this road yesterday and found it empty. Why did she think the path so much better today?

Especially when Mike was asking her to stay.

Her brain churned and her stomach roiled. She could have both the job and the inheritance. She could have the title, the prestige, the money. She could quit being visitor, have friends and a settled life, everything she ever wanted— in Boston.

Except Mike.

Except Andie.

Except wedding planning.

Oh, God, she actually liked wedding planning.

Suddenly, leaving Birch Harbor seemed like the worst decision she'd ever made. Mike had asked her to stay.

But she didn't want to be a visitor in his life. She wanted the fairytale.

Leaving the keys on the worktable and the door unlocked, she ran outside and started jogging toward Hobart & Hobart Auto Repair. By the time she got there, she was sweating. No wonder. Probably eighty degrees already.

She stopped to catch her breath. This was it. Everything was coming out now. Whatever was going on between her and Mike was being laid on the table today.

The overhead garage doors were open, and she spotted Mike and Dan standing next to a blue car, talking. Stomach fluttering, she entered the garage, her footsteps on the cement floor announcing her arrival.

Mike turned. "Delaney?"

She met his eyes. Her pulse quickened. Every word she'd thought to say evaporated from her mind.

"Um, do you need something?" Dan asked in the awkward silence.

Eyes still locked on Mike's, she shifted her feet, suddenly terrified of the pending conversation. "Oil change," she blurted. "I need an oil change."

"You need an oil change?" Mike lifted a brow.

Tell him. She opened her mouth. "And a filter, too," came out.

"We're booked solid. It'll be a while," Dan said.

"I don't think you have time to wait," Mike added.

"Sure. I can wait. Doesn't need to be today. Next week will be soon enough." Her voice trembled and she clenched her teeth together to keep her jaw steady.

"If you leave the car, how are you getting to the airport?" Dan asked.

She didn't answer, just looked at Mike. Just watched him watch her.

Dan cleared his throat and took a few steps backward. "I guess I'll go ... and organize the ... job orders for today. In the office. If you, uh, need me or anything."

When he was gone, Mike asked, "How *are* you getting to the airport?"

"Well ..." She waved a hand. "It's just that I'm not going to the airport. Not anymore."

He waited, his eyes never leaving her face.

"Maybe we should take a walk," she said.

"I don't know. The last time you asked me to take a walk, I didn't like the news."

She huffed. "Humor me."

Five minutes and a couple of blocks later, Delaney finally got up the nerve to say what she'd come to say. "I've ... There are so many people who need help planning their weddings."

Mike nodded.

"I don't want to leave them in the lurch."

They cut through the park and onto a narrow path in the woods, the same path she'd chased Mike down on many a childhood summer day. He fell into step behind her.

"The thing is, I've visited a lot of places in my life. Places ... and relationships. And it's getting old," she said over her shoulder.

"Always on the outside, never the one who belongs."

She nodded even though he couldn't see her face. "And it didn't matter before. It didn't. Until you kissed me."

"Delaney ..."

She stopped beside a big old maple tree. "And I may be about as dumb as I can possibly be to even think that what we have could be real, because my mother, you know, spent a whole lifetime searching." She looked up at the canopy of green above them. "I heard something once, something like, marriage kills love and—"

"Are we talking about love here?"

She brought her eyes to his. *Were* they? Her heart started to pound. This was her moment of truth. *She* was talking about love. What if he wasn't? What if he'd asked her to stay, and he was just talking about lust or friendship or love, maybe someday? What if she was wrong about this bachelor next door?

She pressed a hand to her chest "I don't want to belong just anywhere. I want to belong with you."

He didn't say anything.

"I can't leave ... because I love you." Her voice sped up. "Unless, of course, you don't love me, then, no problem, I can leave ... in complete mortification, just like when I was seventeen." She glanced at the path behind them, her cheeks beginning to burn.

Mike started to laugh, then stopped. "Delaney, I can't say whether you belonged with me when you were seventeen. But I can tell you this—you belong with me now."

A wide smile broke across her face. "I do?"

"Yes." He pulled her into his arms and kissed her until

she could hardly breathe. "I love you," he murmured against her mouth.

"Do you know recognize this tree?" She pointed up at the maple.

He grimaced. "I was hoping you didn't. It's the one Dan and I left you tied to for three hours when you were eight."

"But you came back for me." Her voice caught and she cleared her throat. "Will you always? No matter what? Will you always come back for me?"

"Count on it." He kissed her again. "Now, about that wedding-planning business ..."

Delaney rested her hands on his chest. "If I'm really going to make a go of it, I've got to book some more weddings."

"I know one you could get started on right away. They haven't picked a date yet, but you could help with that, too."

"Who?"

"All I know is, the wedding has to be filled with enchantment because that's what brought them together."

He couldn't possibly be saying what she hoped he was saying. "It sounds perfect for Storybook Weddings! Who's getting married?"

He dropped kisses on each of her cheeks, her eyelids, her nose and, finally, her mouth. "We are," he said. And he kissed her again.

EPILOGUE

"THIS CELEBRATION GETS WILDER EVERY YEAR," Delaney said.

Holding hands, she and Mike walked across their backyard where a party was in full swing.

"Happy anniversary, you two." Stonewall raised his beer in toast.

"Happy tenth anniversary, sweetheart." Mike squeezed Delaney's hand.

She leaned in to kiss him.

"I like this," Dan called from his chair on the deck. "Ten years, three kids, and still public displays of affection." He bent to kiss Lauren.

Mike grinned. "The first party was the best," he said.

They'd married later that first summer, after the other weddings were over, the band shell finished, the summer concert series booked and the '57 Chevy restored and driven in the Fourth of July parade.

Once everyone learned what Aunt Ellie had been trying to do, they all were determined to meet the terms of the will even though they didn't have to. The Henrys had even quit fighting—most of the time.

The party was a tradition now. An anniversary of their wedding, the will, and the legacy left by Ellie Clark—a celebration that tied them all together.

"Hey, Dad." Andie fell into step beside them. "Can I take the car to the beach tomorrow? Everyone wants to go one more time before we head back to college."

Mike looked at Delaney.

"It's all yours, sweetie," she said. "Have fun." She watched Andie head back toward a group of her friends. Love filled her heart and she looked at Mike. "The first was wonderful, you're right. But I think I like this one best."

"You say that every year." Mike nuzzled his wife's hair.

"That's because every passing year reminds me that we've found happily-ever-after. And as it turns out, that's all I ever really wanted, after all."

———

If you enjoyed this book … I would be forever grateful if you would post a review on the site where you bought it.

———

The third book in the Bachelor Next Door series, **BREATHLESS ON THE BOULEVARD**, is Nora's story. Please enjoy the following excerpt.

———

Excerpt from
BREATHLESS ON THE BOULEVARD
The Bachelor Next Door, book three

Chapter One

Nora Clark knew she was in trouble the moment she heard her sister's voice on the phone. "Tell me I just misunderstood you," she said. "Tell me this connection is so bad you didn't really say what I think I just heard."

"It's the only answer," Tess replied. "You have to take my place."

"Don't be ridiculous. We're not kids anymore. This isn't a game." Nora tightened her grip on the phone, paced across her small kitchen, and looked out at her tiny San Francisco backyard.

She'd been supporting her sister for two years as she tried to build a personal shopping business. Now Tess wanted Nora to *be* the personal shopper? Enough was enough. "Look, Tess, when your new, important client wants you to do a rush job for her son, the correct answer is, you get off that cruise ship and come home."

"I'm on the Inside Passage, remember? Alaska? Open water. Icebergs. You don't just jump off cruise ships up here. Besides, I can't desert Liza. She only came along because I begged her to." Tess's voice turned pleading. "Please, Nora ... I can't afford to lose this account. Camille

Lamont is such a famous author. She's so connected, she could totally make my career. I can't say no."

"This is *your* business, not mine," Nora said through gritted teeth. "If you want to help ... this guy—"

"Erik. His mom said his name is Erik."

"If you want to help Erik, you need to figure this out your—"

"I'm trying to. But I'm telling you, there's no way off this ship except via emergency helicopter. And I doubt that shopping counts as an emergency. Please, Nora. He'll never know you're not me. We're completely identical—"

"Tess, this is beyond stupid—"

"No, no, it's smart actually. Think about it. If I make Camille happy, she'll give me referrals, referrals mean I make more money. And more money means I get out of your hair—not to mention your house—sooner." Tess paused. "Maybe then you'd have time to date."

"Tess!"

"Nora!" Her sister mimicked her annoyed tone.

"Okay, fine, I'll go to the appointment ... and explain that you're on a seventeen-day cruise—"

"No! What will Camille think when she learns I sent someone who knows *next to nothing* about personal shopping to meet with her son?" Tess groaned. "I can see this account waving goodbye already. You have to be me. Just pretend you're me."

"Absolutely not. Either tell her the truth or come back to San Francisco and meet with her yourself," Nora said as evenly as possible. "It's called re-spon-si-bility."

"We're practically in grizzly territory up here. Probably polar bear, too."

Nora let out a snort. "I doubt the bear populations will be attacking you at the next port of call—or the airport, for that matter."

"Nora." Tess's voice dropped low. "When Keegan called off our wedding, I thought I would die. I need this cruise. Even *you* said it was a good idea. The Lamont account is important to me, but I'm just not up to it yet. I've only been on the ship one day. What kind of a respite is that?"

Nora dropped into a kitchen chair as she tried to reason everything out. Tess had really hit bottom when Keegan dumped her. And though Nora had never been able to understand her sister's devastation over losing that idiot, she'd agreed that time away might help Tess heal. Especially since their cousin Liza—the epitome of responsible—had agreed to go along. Maybe she'd rub off on Tess.

Besides the cruise had already been paid for—it was supposed to have been Tess and Keegan's honeymoon.

Even so, that didn't mean Nora taking her place was a good idea. "Tess, we may look the same but that's where the similarity ends. I'm a physical therapist. You're a personal shopper. You're loose and carefree. I'm ... not."

"I'll say."

"What?"

"Sorry. Sorry."

"Anyway, pretending to be you, even for one meeting, is like ... expecting apples to be oranges."

"You didn't used to be an apple. You just became one over the years."

"I did not." Indignation rose up inside her.

"Then why do you keep staying in that hospital physical therapy job when you hate it? Come on, I know your complaints by heart." Tess's voice took on a singsong quality. "Once people have surgery, all you do is make sure they can use a walker and get out of a chair, and then—boom!—they're gone. Discharged. You never get to see rehab through to the end."

"It's important work," Nora said.

Tess kept talking. "And what about that new sports medicine rehab center the hospital's opening? They have to hire someone—have you even applied yet?"

The truth in her words irritated Nora more than the know-it-all tone of her voice. "Tess, when people grow up they discover you can't have everything. You become—"

"Dull. But you don't have to."

Nora slowly counted to ten in her head. "Whatever. My pretending to be you is still beyond stupid. Switching places is something you do when you're seventeen."

"Or something you do when your sister really needs your help. This isn't about Erik Lamont and you know it. It's about keeping his mother happy. If she wants me to do a quick job for her son, I can't *not* do it." She let out an exaggerated sigh. "Nora—she'll hire someone else."

"Couldn't you just call her and explain that—"

"Nora? Hello? Hello? You're breaking up."

"Tess? Can you hear me?"

Silence greeted Nora's words, and she raised her eyes to the ceiling in frustration. Pressing redial, she kicked into her spiel again as soon as Tess answered. "Just tell Camille you're on a long cruise in Alaska. Surely she'll understand that people take vacations." She pressed the fingers of one hand to her forehead.

"I don't want to risk it—she's too new a client. How hard could it be to take my place just this once? Help me out with Erik Lamont." Tess let out a laugh. "You never know, he could be cute ..."

"Not even funny." Nora stood, unable to stay seated long with the conversation twisting and turning the way that it was.

"Why do you always discount the possibility of meeting another man? Kevin died five years ago—"

"How did we get from me impersonating you to my getting hooked up with some guy we don't even know, and for all we know is an unemployed loser living off his mother or still in high school or something? Tess, sometimes you're like a broken record."

"So will you take my place?"

Nora huffed. "New song. Same broken record. No. How could I? What if his mom notices the difference?"

"Why would his mom be there? You're shopping for him."

"Well, his mom made the call. Really, Tess, I'd help you if I could." She felt a tugging at the back of her shirt and turned to smile at her five-year-old son.

"Mama," Danny said. "I think I found a new daddy—the right one. Come." He pulled her with him toward the living room.

Tess kept talking into her ear. "Yeah, well, what happens if I tell his mother I can't do it?"

"Hold on a minute, Tess." She looked at Danny. "What?"

"I found a new daddy on TV." His brown eyes shone with earnestness.

"You can't just find a daddy on TV. It's not that easy."

"But you said if I found one to let you know."

Nora sighed. Whatever had possessed her to say such a thing to him?

"He's really nice." Danny pointed at the television where Mr. Rogers was cutting construction paper with scissors and talking in his perfectly calm voice.

"Mr. Rogers? Oh, Danny, Mr. Rogers is—" *Dead.* "Uh—married already. Tell you what, sweetie, why don't you go get a cookie and I'll be off in a minute." She watched him dash into the kitchen, then turned her attention back to the phone.

"Something wrong?" Tess asked.

"He's looking for a daddy again. Found one on TV that he thinks is just right. *Mr. Rogers.*"

"God, he's really getting determined about that. Maybe you should sign up for some online dating—"

"Stop."

Danny hopped into the room munching on a cookie and she went back into the kitchen.

"Okay," Tess said. "So I was saying, what happens if I turn this job down and Camille finds some other personal shopper who is ready and willing to help. Then she thinks, *Wow, I like this new on-the-ball shopper girl who's available whenever I need her. I think I'll give her all my business.* Just like that, I'll have lost my biggest account. All because I didn't meet with—"

Suddenly, silence was all Nora heard, and she knew the connection had dropped again. "Damn!" she muttered. She set her phone on the counter and stared at the cupboard, noticing for the first time all the dried milk spatters on the dark wood doors.

How did all this milk splash up here? And how could she not have seen it before? She grabbed the dishrag from the sink and began to wipe off the doors as she debated whether or not to call Tess back.

Her head felt like it was going to burst. She knew this account was crucial to Tess's success, to Tess making enough money to support herself, *to Tess ever moving out of Nora's house.* She exhaled. Which meant, keeping this account had to be as important to Nora as it was to Tess.

BREATHLESS ON THE BOULEVARD excerpt
Copyright © 2017 by Pamela Ford

ABOUT THE AUTHOR

PAMELA FORD is the award-winning author of contemporary and historical romance. She grew up watching old movies, blissfully sighing over the romance; and reading sci-fi and adventure novels, vicariously living the action. The combination probably explains why the books she writes are romantic, happily-ever-afters with plenty of plot—and often, lots of laughter.

After graduating from college with a degree in Advertising, Pam spent many years as a copywriter and freelance writer before inserting a plot twist in her career path and writing her first book.

Pam has won numerous awards including the Booksellers Best, the Laurel Wreath, and a gold medal IPPY in the Independent Book Publisher Awards. She is a National Readers' Choice Awards finalist, a Maggie Awards finalist, a Kindle Book Awards finalist, and a two-time Golden Heart Finalist. More than a half million copies of her books have been sold worldwide.